Advance Praise for *Zek*

"[Zek] strikes me as an honest, accurate account of imprisonment, and I am especially grateful for the details about solitary. It is a compelling and important novel."

—Katy Ryan, West Virginia University, Associate Professor of English and Founder of the Appalachian Prison Book Project (APBP)

"America's deranged experiment with mass incarceration has generated a continuing fascination in the media. Television shows like Prison Break, Oz, and Orange is the New Black have dramatized the prison experience for millions of viewers. Arthur Longworth's Zek provides an insider's account of prison life that is every bit as compelling as these shows, but with a depth that goes beyond what television can offer. It is a remarkable effort."

—Miguel Ferguson, Ph.D., Associate Professor, University of Texas School of Social Work, and founder of "Words Beyond Walls," a prisoner/student education program

Zek

An American Prison Story

Arthur Longworth

Gabalfa Press
Seattle

Zek: An American Prison Story.

Published by Gabalfa Press, Seattle.

for all inquiries, please email
publisher@gabalfapress.com

www.gabalfapress.com

ISBN 978-0-9970299-0-1

Cover Photo and Design,
Raw Love Productions
www.rawloveproductions.com

Zek (zek) n. Russian slang for prisoner in the Gulag.

Prologue

The prisoner lay quiet on the narrow steel bunk as guards stripped a cell not far down the tier. He could not see them, only the whitewashed wall outside the bars of the cell he was in, but his ears followed what they were doing.

Earlier in the day, a squad of guards in body armor and helmets forcibly extracted the cell's occupant spraying him through the bars of his cell with a burning, oil-based chemical that adhered to his skin. Once he faltered, the guards entered the cell and shocked him senseless with a Taser gun. Then they dragged him out, pinned him facedown with their boots and knees, and shackled his wrists and ankles behind him in a hog-tied fashion. Afterward, they hauled him to another tier on the block and put him into a *strip-cell.*

This was the standard course of action for dealing with a prisoner who refuses the order to kneel on the yellow line at the front of his cell. In this section of the prison, *the Hole,* forcible extractions were commonplace events.

He heard the guards step out of the cell and onto the tier. It hadn't taken them long. He supposed that was because each cell only enclosed a five-by-seven-foot space, most of which was taken up by a concrete bunk and steel toilet. Not much to strip out.

When the trudge of bootfalls receded down the tier, he rose and stood at the front of his cell looking out through the bars. Twenty feet away, nearly beyond his line of sight, lay a thin plastic bunk pad thrown against the wall. Beside it was a worn sheet and state blanket stained yellow by the burning chemical, the discoloration of the bedding interrupted by a dark spattering of blood.

His eyes stopped on a book, half-buried beneath the blanket. Only a thin paperback volume—and the fact that it was beneath the blanket would only make it harder for him to get—but the sight buoyed his spirit. He was on *ISO* and it had been more than six months since they had allowed him anything to read.

He turned his attention to the waistband of his state-issue briefs, searching for the spot where its threads were loosest. He began to pluck at one. The undershorts were all that he wore because no air circulated in the cell (no air circulated in any cell in that place). Wearing anything else would only cause him to perspire worse than he already was. Besides, a pair of coveralls was the only other clothing item prisoners in that place were issued and he had grown accustomed to using the threadbare pair they had given him as a pillow.

He pulled the first thread from the waistband slowly, being careful not to break it. The ones after it came more easily. When he had collected enough, he knotted them together end to end.

He removed a small plastic comb from beneath his bunk pad and went to the back wall of the cell. Utilizing the comb, he picked something out of a crack that divided the wall from floor to ceiling in a jagged, meandering line. Returning to the bunk, he tied the comb to the line he had made from the thread. Then, holding the small object from the crack between his thumb and forefinger, he examined it closely. It was fashioned from three tiny staples, each bent into a hook and bound to the others by thread. Adjusting the hooks until they were equal distance apart, he folded the object out into what looked like a miniature grappling hook. Taking up the line again, he tied the hook to the comb.

Rising from the bunk, he slid his sweat-slick arms out through the bars, clasping the comb and hook lightly in one hand and the line to which they were attached in the other. Gauging the distance carefully, he cast.

He made several dozen attempts before he was able to catch a good hold on the book and pull it down the tier and into his cell. Looking at what remained of its cover, he realized it was about prison—specifically, a day in the life of some prisoner. He felt a twinge of disappointment. He had never read a story about prison that wasn't bullshit—written by someone who had never lived a day inside—a fairy tale, replete with storybook ending. Not the way things really were. He noted that the author's name was foreign (the last name unpronounceable). He doubted the man could know what it was like to be in a prison in this country, in a prison like he was in.

He knew if the guards caught him with the book he would get more ISO time. But he dismissed the thought as soon as it came to him. The truth was that he didn't believe there was anything left they could threaten him with. He had lived in that place for a long time—all of his adult life, in fact—and he had experienced far worse things there than ISO. Even if the book was bullshit, now that he had it, he knew he would not relinquish it willingly under any circumstance. If they wanted it, they would have to do to him what they had done to the prisoner down the tier.

Sitting down on the bunk, he opened the book to

its first page and stared down at the words. After a moment's hesitation, he began to read.

Several hours later, he let the book's cover close but continued to stare at it for some time. Any other book he would have rationed—reading a page or two at a time, holding himself to only enough per day to keep his mind from eroding, yet still have more to read for the next day—that was the way he had learned to do it in that place. He had found that it wasn't possible with this book, though.

He set the book down slowly, almost reverentially, and rose from the bunk. He began to pace the length of the cell—two-and-a-half steps in one direction and two-and-a-half in the other. Reading the book had triggered something inside him, although he didn't yet understand what.

Finally, after more than an hour, he sat down again. Reaching beneath the plastic bunk pad, he brought out a pen and what remained of a yellow legal tablet. He didn't have much paper, but he believed that if he wrote small enough...

Setting the legal tablet on his thigh, he touched the pen to the paper. After a moment's hesitation, he began to write.

The Day

A sudden deluge of light pierced Jonny's eyelids as if they didn't exist, causing him to squint and bring a hand up to cover them. His peaceful, sleeping countenance was shattered. That was the disadvantage of having a top bunk—the cell light was on the ceiling less than three feet from his face.

The light was turned on every morning at this time—5:45 a.m.—and Jonny had lived under its harsh glare long enough that he did not remember any other way to wake up. No matter how accustomed to living in that place he had become, though, the light was something he never got used to.

His body was wracked by a sudden fit of coughing, and he wondered what was wrong with him. He had been coughing for two days, and it had carried over through most of last night as well.

When the cough abated, he opened his eyes, keeping them narrowed against the light, and glanced around at his three *cellies*. They were still asleep, seemingly oblivious to the light and the sound of his coughing.

He lifted the worn state blanket that covered him over his head in an attempt to shut out the light. It didn't cut it off completely, and came at the cost of exposing his sockless feet to the cold of the cell, but it did provide enough relief that he was able to relax his eyelids.

He lay unmoving on the narrow steel bunk and listened. The giant, old, brick cell-house was silent. But soon he knew it would be transformed into an unebbing sea of noise. Unlike the light, though, he was used to that.

He contemplated the soreness of his throat and wondered if he should sign up for sick call. But, even as he thought this, he knew it was not really an option. He had never been inclined to go to the infirmary—he knew too many prisoners who had died there, or who had returned to the cellblock much more damaged than they were before they left. That was also where they had conducted the radiation experiments—and the way he saw it, people who would zap a prisoner's nuts full of radiation just to see what would happen, were not the kind of people he trusted. Besides, getting on the sick-call list would cost him money and that was something he did not have. He decided that, whatever was wrong with him, he would have to ride it out.

The distant sounds of laughter and the clank of keys came to him as a trio of guards entered the block and began the long trudge up the stairs that led to the top tier of the three-story cell-house. That was where Jonny and his cellies lived—in cell E-14, third cell from the end—and guards began the count every morning at the end of their tier. He did not know if they were told to do it that way, or if it was just something that had been passed down since the beginning, from one guard to another over the 122 years that the prison had existed. It was the only way he remembered them ever doing it.

He heard the sound of a count-board being slapped against the bars of the cell next door. "Bunk three!

Move for count!"

Jonny pulled the blanket away from his face while the guard yelled at his neighbor. He didn't want to give them a reason to say anything to him. The guards moved in front of the cell and took quick inventory, then moved on. Jonny stole a look over the edge of the bunk in order to make sure Matt wasn't awake, then sat up and pushed the blanket off himself. Swinging his legs over the side, he slid off the bunk and landed lightly on the cold concrete floor. Retreating to the rear of the cell, he began to pull on a set of prison-issue clothing. It didn't bother him that the ill-fitting khaki trousers and work shirt were the same that he had worn the previous day, and the day before that. Sometimes he wore the same clothes for a week. Many prisoners there did, because doing laundry was a bitch. It had to be done in a five-gallon plastic bucket inside of their eight-by-ten-foot cell. Then, of course, he would have to find room to hang it up to dry in a space that was already too small for the four people that lived in it.

Gathering his towel and soap dish, Jonny set them on the end of one of the footlockers protruding from beneath Matt's bunk. He placed a worn pair of plastic shower shoes on the floor next to the cell door and turned to look at the two bunks on the other side of the cell. On the lower one was a mountain of snoring flesh under a state blanket rendered small in comparison to what was beneath it. This was Corey, and Jonny knew that he would remain like he was for as long as he could. It was his day off from where he worked in the prison bakery and, after a week of getting up at 4:00 a.m., it was his habit to sleep in.

The smaller lump on the upper bunk was another story. This was Seth, the youngster, and he always slept as long as he could because that is just the way youngsters who feel they have nothing left to get up for are. He had shown up five months earlier, fresh off *the chain bus*, and they had let him move in to take the bunk of their old cellie who had gone to the Hole (and was later transferred to *the Bay*) for a fight in the Chowhall. Jonny checked the urge to wake him. The kid would learn soon enough, he thought, and the fifty-three years the judge had sentenced him to would certainly be enough time for him to do it.

Using the end of his footlocker as a step, Jonny launched himself up onto his bunk and lay down again. He rested the crook of his arm over his eyes in order to block the light, and felt the bunk shake as Matt stirred below. He heard the soft slap of his cellie's bare feet hit the floor.

The cell-house loudspeakers crackled loudly and came to life. "B Tier! Showers!"

"Damn." Jonny swore under his breath, experiencing his first flicker of agitation of the day. Their tier was supposed to be first, although the guards screwing up the schedule was not anything new. He sat up and reached out to the bars, flipping their sign out. Each of the 102 cells in the cell-house had a sign with a number painted on it fastened to its bars. When the sign was extended outward, the guard in the security booth overlooking the block knew that a prisoner in the cell wanted out. The security booth was in control of the opening and closing of all cell doors in the block, although Jonny knew the guard posted there would not open until showers were called for the tier. He lay back down to wait, returning the crook of his arm over his eyes.

The cell-house had come alive with sound, its volume increasing as more prisoners got up. An argument erupted in a cell on one of the tiers below Jonny's. He tried hard to focus only on the sound of Matt splashing water on his face in the back of their cell, but he was unable to ignore what he heard.

"Nigga, you ain't cleaned yo'self in a week! Get the fuck down to the shower and wash yo' ass!"

"Fuck you, nigga! Worry 'bout yo'self! Ain't no mutha'fucka' gonna tell me what to do up in here!"

"Yo' filthy, nigga! Yo, filthy! Ya' need to go on n' find yo'self anotha' place to live! The rest of us, we don't like livin' up in here with no filthy niggas—mutha'fucka's who won't even clean theyselves!"

"I ain't movin' nowhere! You's the one who needs to move!"

"Brothas! Brothas! Why you putting your business out on the tier like this?" A calming voice of reason called over from another cell. Jonny recognized it as belonging to a Muslim elder who lived nearby. This was not the first time he had interceded between these two. Their early morning arguments were starting to become routine.

"Where you working today?" Matt asked him in a quiet voice. Despite the noise outside the cell, he was conscious that Corey and Seth were still asleep.

"One Wing," Jonny answered, not taking his arm off of his eyes.

"If you run into Hawk over there, would you tell him to meet me on the Yard tonight?"

"Sure."

Jonny didn't mind doing things for Matt. They had known each other since the beginning of this and got along well. Besides, he knew that his friend would be stuck in the metal plant all day cranking out license plates. It was what he did every day.

Matt was from Seattle, too, so, in a way, he was Jonny's homeboy, although Jonny never would have considered him that before he came to prison. He was from a well-off neighborhood that overlooked Puget Sound, on the north end of the city. Very different from the public housing that Jonny had grown up in with his mother and younger sister. Someone coming to prison from Matt's neighborhood was an aberration. There were areas of Seattle from which a lot of people were sent to prison, but the neighborhood Matt was from wasn't one of them. In his neighborhood, anyone who didn't graduate high school and go on to a university was considered an oddball, a failure. Someone from there being sent to prison with a sixty-year sentence, like Matt had, was something that Jonny doubted had ever happened before.

Jonny had met him ten years earlier when they were in the county jail together, each facing long prison sentences. He supposed it was their age that had drawn them together initially. At the time, he was seventeen, and Matt eighteen. After that, it was the shared experience of what they went through that enabled them to bridge the gap between the different worlds they were from.

Not many prisoners knew what Matt was in for, but Jonny knew exactly what they said he had done. Matt's girlfriend was found dead behind the high school they went to and, because of his connection to her, police immediately focused their investigation on him. Shortly afterward, they arrested him. At trial, the prosecutor told the jury that Matt had become upset when his girlfriend dumped him and began going out with someone else. He said Matt waited in ambush outside the school and, when he saw her walking on the wooded trail along which he knew she passed every day, he hit her over the head with a rock and killed her. Although there were no witnesses to the crime, the prosecutor produced a friend of Matt's to testify that Matt had confessed to him what he had done. At the time of his testimony, the friend was facing unrelated charges that, after the trial, were of course dropped.

Matt had always sworn to Jonny that he didn't do it, a fact that caused Jonny more pause for thought after ten years in prison than he had when his friend first said it. After all, nearly everyone in jail swears to their innocence but, after being convicted and spending years in prison, there are not many who continue to insist on it. Jonny had seen it enough times over the years. There nearly always comes a point after coming to prison when a guy begins to admit his guilt, no matter how unwilling or unable he is at first. But Matt had never done that. Jonny even prodded him from time to time in order to see if he would, but he never came close.

Jonny wasn't sure whether Matt realized it, but it didn't matter to him if he did the crime or not. He wouldn't have condemned him for it. He couldn't because he knew firsthand what it was to be guilty of a violent, impulsive act that ended in an ugly, inalterable consequence. His own *beef* was testament to that.

The door of the cell jerked and shuddered suddenly as it began to grind open—the sound a combination of the dull drone of an electric motor and the grating rasp of heavy steel bars sliding along gritty, ungreased steel runners.

"B Tier! Showers!"

The sound of the door and loudspeaker snapped Jonny away from his thoughts. He launched himself from the bunk and slipped quickly into his shower shoes. Snatching up his towel and soap dish, he ducked out of the cell and took off down the tier.

He moved fast because he knew the showers would already be crowded and he didn't want to be behind any more people than he had to be. Living at the end of the tier was a disadvantage, but he had become adept at dealing with it. The tier was less than three feet wide and it wasn't possible to pass anyone on it, so the trick was to do precisely what he was doing—exit his cell and proceed down the tier as quickly as possible. While others were still scrambling to get out of their bunks, he was passing their cell. Not everyone could be had that easily though. He ran into a line of prisoners in front of 6 *House* and fell in behind them.

The guard in the security booth shouted over the loudspeakers. "Walk! Slow your asses down or I'll send all of you back!"

A disjointed chorus of convict voices from around the cellblock responded. "Fuck you, motherfucker!"

"Bring your coward ass out of the booth and say

that, bitch!"

"Tell your mother to slow down!"

Jonny slowed slightly. He knew it was important to make at least that gesture. Once he got through the gate at the head of the tier, the guard would no longer be a concern—they would be out of his sight and beyond his range of electronic control. Until that point though, he could slam the gate and seal them on the tier, leaving no other place for them to go but back to their cells.

When Jonny made it through the gate, he quickened his pace, taking advantage of an opportunity to pass two less-determined prisoners before making it to the stairs.

The stairs were as narrow as the tier, but progress was slower there because traffic moved in both directions—prisoners returning from the showers made their way up, squeezing past the line of prisoners on their way down. Taking the steel-and-concrete stairs fast would not have been a good idea anyway—the passage of so many soaked shower shoes always left them slick. Jonny moved with the descending stream of people.

At the bottom of the stairs, he sped up again. Steering around a group of prisoners gathered in front of the guards' office, he moved toward a heavy steel door at the back of the cell-house. A number of prisoners loitered outside it, waiting. This wasn't a strategy to which Jonny subscribed. He had been in too long to let crowded conditions deter him from anything. He knew that the only way for a prisoner to get what he had coming in that place was for him to wade in without hesitating and lay claim to it. Those too new to know that, or too meek to assert themselves, didn't have anything coming. That's just the way it was.

Pulling the heavy steel door open, Jonny found himself facing a wall of flesh through which there seemed no possible way to pass.

"Excuse me," he said, loud enough to be heard over the sound of the showers and multitude of voices. It was a general declaration not addressed to anyone in particular. Choosing a point in the pressing mass that he judged to be the most susceptible to admission, he moved to wedge his way in.

Amid the mob of naked and half-naked prisoners in the shower room, he navigated carefully so as not to step on any feet or brush against anyone too roughly (at least not anyone fully naked, because even in that place that was not something that was considered acceptable). Reaching a bench piled high with clothing and towels, he began to take off his clothes. It was one of two benches in the room: one belonging to white prisoners, the other to blacks. Other race groups had to choose which bench they would use according to whom they were most closely affiliated with. Winter blasted into the room through half a dozen large vents. The icy air was meant to force out the steam, but seemed only to serve the purpose of making the room every bit as cold as it was outside.

Jonny shed his clothing with practiced efficiency, although doing it here was more difficult than it would have been elsewhere because being crowded in on all sides gave him little room to work with. Rolling his clothes into a bundle with his towel outermost, he placed them atop the chaos on the bench. To the uninitiated, it would appear a hopeless jumble, but the reality was quite different. Everyone in the shower room knew precisely where their things were and how they had laid them there.

Jonny turned toward the showerheads set close together along the back wall of the room (there were fifteen, although only twelve actually worked). Through the crowd, he saw his friend Claude standing under the one in the corner. He was waiting for him.

"Excuse me." Jonny made his way around other prisoners waiting for a chance to get under a shower.

"Thanks, bro," he said, as he stepped into the stream of water his friend had just stepped out of. The shower was now his. That was the way things were done there—prisoners looking out for each other took precedence over those who simply waited their turn (unless, of course, they were weak enough to be challenged, in which case an entirely different dynamic would come into play).

The water was warm and silenced Jonny's teeth, which had begun to chatter from the cold, although it felt a long way from warming him completely. The narrow spray only hit one part of him at a time, while the rest remained exposed to the frigid, blasting air. He moved around beneath the nozzle for a full minute in order to get every part of himself wet. Then, stepping aside, he nodded to another prisoner, giving him permission to take a turn under the water while he soaped himself up. Everyone shared showers in that same fashion (some with as many as five prisoners between a single shower head). With so many people waiting and so few showers, it was the only way to do it.

Jonny began to lather himself, starting with his head. He kept it shaved—most prisoners there did—because it was easier. His hand passed over the long scar on the right side of his abdomen. This was where they had opened him up in order to retrieve the bullet that had lodged against the inside of one of his ribs—a 9mm memento bestowed upon him by the Seattle police.

Looking around the room, he was struck by how crowded it was—literally wall-to-wall bodies. Although he was accustomed to it, he was aware of the effect it had on those who were new in the prison. When *ducks* entered the shower room for the first time, the look on their faces (of astonishment, disbelief, and horror) was always clear to see. Often it was a long time before they were able to work up enough nerve to return. Jonny knew that was what was going on with Seth. Despite how long he had been there, he still only made it down to the showers once every three or four days. It was something he was going to have to get over, Jonny thought. Time he hardened up. Their cell was too close of quarters for one of them to be in there smelling bad.

As he worked the soap into his armpits, Jonny spotted a duck in the crowd waiting for a shower. He had to be a duck because he was on the wrong side of the room. Seeing that fewer people were waiting on the black side, he was trying to get in over there despite the fact he was white. Watching him, Jonny realized it didn't matter—as timid as the guy looked, he wouldn't be able to get a shower on either side. Other prisoners kept stepping in front of him and crowding him out, and the duck didn't say or do anything about it. Jonny could not find it in his heart to feel sorry for the guy, who he thought looked to be somewhere near his own age. Fact was, they sent guys there who were still teenagers (they had done it to him!), and some of them found a way to make it. Why should he have any sympathy for a motherfucker like this? If he wasn't able to get a shower (or anything else, for that matter), it didn't make a difference to him.

A loud clanging resounded through the room—the sound of steel struck against steel. Jonny stepped back beneath his shower in order to rinse off. He and the others around him knew that the banging on the door was the two-minute warning from the guard outside. After a moment under the water, he stepped out so one of the prisoners still waiting could have the shower for the time that remained.

After Jonny had dried himself and was about to pull a t-shirt over his head, he noticed that everyone had a shower except for the duck, who stood in the center of the shower-room floor looking frustrated. Jonny realized he wasn't the only one who didn't feel sorry for him.

When he was fully dressed, Jonny steered around other prisoners still dressing and pushed open the door. As he stepped back out into the relative warmth of the cellblock, he heard the cascading hiss of the showers cease abruptly. That was it—showers were over.

A steady line of prisoners filed down the stairs

and passed through the metal detector in front of the guards' office. Jonny realized he would have to hurry if he wanted to eat—they had begun to run tiers to chow.

Climbing the narrow stairs against traffic with his towel and soap dish in hand, he felt as though he were fighting the current of a river. At the top, traffic eased and he was able to move faster. Arriving on his tier, he heard the loud click and hum of the loudspeaker.

"E Tier! Mainline!"

"Shit." Jonny broke into a shuffle (the only way he was able to move quickly with shower shoes on) and made it to the front of his cell just as the cell doors began to roll open.

Matt and Corey stepped out onto the tier fully dressed.

"Better hurry, bro," Matt said, as Jonny brushed past him into the cell. "You want us to wait?"

"No, go on. I'll make it," Jonny told him, tossing his wet towel over the end of his bunk and kicking off the shower shoes.

Seth dressed hurriedly on the other side of the cell. It was obvious he had awakened only seconds earlier.

Jonny grabbed his coat off the post at the end of his bunk and snatched up a pair of work boots from the floor. Slipping quickly back out of the cell, he sat down on the concrete tier and began to pull on the worn pair of socks that had been tucked inside the boots.

"Coming closed!" The loudspeaker barked as the entire tier of cell doors began to roll shut.

Seth lunged toward the door and managed to make it through wearing only one shoe, the other in his hand. He was a big kid—over six feet tall and two hundred pounds—and had come within an inch of being caught by the heavy barred door.

He'll learn when he gets closed in it, Jonny thought, shaking his head. Anyone that happened to was taken to the Hole.

"Damn," Seth swore and turned back to the cell. He

inserted his arm through the bars and tried to grab hold of the state-issue coat that lay on his bunk, just out of reach.

"You aren't ever going to learn how to do this, are you?" Jonny said, cinching his bootlaces tight and pushing himself up off the floor. "Put your shoes on," he told the younger prisoner as he exchanged places with him at the bars.

Reaching into the cell, Jonny grabbed the end of the mattress pad and pulled it toward him. The youngster was still tying his shoes when Jonny pulled the coat through the bars and turned to wait for him.

Jonny believed Seth would be a good convict once he got the hang of it. He was going to be bigger than his brother when he was fully grown, Jonny judged, as he watched him tie his shoes.

Jonny knew Seth's older brother, Brady, although he had never particularly cared for him. Corey and Matt knew him too, from the last time he was in prison. That had been just over a year earlier. And it hadn't been long after his release that they had read about him in the newspaper. Brady had been arrested for leaning out of a car window and firing a shotgun into a vehicle whose driver had apparently looked at him in a way that he didn't like. Seth was driving the car Brady fired from, so the county prosecutor offered him a plea deal for twelve years on the condition that he testify against his brother. The youngster refused and, as a consequence, he got the sentence that he had—fifty-three years.

Jonny respected Seth because of that. He, Corey, and Matt had followed the case through the newspaper and they had agreed before he arrived that when Seth got there they would look out for him.

When Seth's shoes were tied, Jonny handed him his coat and they left the tier together. Descending the stairs, they saw three guards standing near the metal detector at the front of the cell-house. Jonny could tell they were laying to search someone and, because he and the youngster were the last two off the tier, there was no doubt it would be one of them.

The guards eyed them as they approached and Jonny was careful not to return their gaze directly. His expression remained impassive. Stepping through the detector, he began to cough loudly, bending forward as the force of it wracked his body. It wasn't hard for him to do. He had a sore throat anyway, so once he got the coughing started, it took over on its own.

The guards looked at Jonny with a mixture of disgust and unease. Ignoring them, he wiped the back of his hand across the underside of his nose as though it were running—even though it wasn't—and then, proceeded on his way.

"Stand for search!"

Jonny didn't hesitate or falter in his step. He knew that the order had been directed at Seth.

At the end of the old cell-house's narrow entrance hall, Jonny pushed open a large steel door and stepped out into a frozen courtyard. It was bitter cold and he could tell from the burning sensation in his nostrils that it was somewhere below zero. He slid a stocking cap from his pocket and put it on, pulling it down as low over his brow as he could while still allowing himself to see. Pushing his hands into the pockets of his coat and being careful not to lose his footing on the ice-covered concrete, he set off across the courtyard in the direction of the large brick building that housed the Chowhall.

When he entered through the wide double doors at the front of the building, Jonny saw that he was in luck—there were not a lot of people still waiting for trays. Passing the line of guards picketed at the entrance, he made his way up the center aisle and added himself to the end of a queue.

The Chowhall enclosed an enormous area. Its ceiling was three stories high and it contained more floor space than an auditorium. A solid wall of noise rose from the hundreds of prisoners who sat at tables on either side of the wide center aisle Jonny stood in. And the tumult wasn't dominated by any one section or group. It didn't consist of anything that by itself could be considered loud, but was instead the agglomeration of all that was taking place there at once. Two lines of prisoners waiting for trays ran side by side down the center and, above them, looking down on the sea of incarcerated beings was a balcony manned by a pair of guards armed with shotguns.

Jonny had seen many people over the years enter this Chowhall for the first time—he had done it himself once—and he knew it was an intimidating experience. When a prisoner walked in wearing the orange coveralls that marked him as a new arrival, the otherwise constant roar would ebb suddenly and every convict there would turn to look at them. It was merely a forbidding place for those who didn't know anybody, a potentially deadly one for anyone who was recognized by an enemy in the crowd. The manner in which a duck carried himself through the experience was watched by a thousand eyes.

"They're always searching me."

Hearing the grumbled complaint, Jonny turned. "What took you so long?"

"The faggots stripped me out," Seth said, his face still pink with anger. "They're always trying to see someone naked... I'm tired of the shit."

Jonny clapped the young prisoner on the shoulder. "It's because you're still new. They'll ease up after awhile."

"I'm tired of the shit," Seth repeated, shaking his head, not placated.

Jonny frowned. He knew that, despite what Seth was saying, the young prisoner couldn't afford to be tired. Not with fifty-two years remaining on his sentence.

When they reached the head of the line, they plucked plastic spoons from a tangle piled on the counter. Jonny checked his for remnants of the previous meal. He decided that it didn't look bad, save for a greasy residue that he rubbed off on his shirt.

At the serving window, Jonny took the brown plastic tray pushed out to him by a prisoner in heavily stained white coveralls. On it was his allotment of what they got every Tuesday, Thursday, and Saturday morning—eggs and toast. Although only a prisoner would have identified it as that. A free person wouldn't have recognized it as such. What passed as eggs there actually started out as yellow powder that was received at the prison in large barrels. Even after it was mixed with water and cooked, it didn't resemble anything that had ever come from a real egg. And the toast was two small pieces of hardened bread. It was put through an aging process instead of being heated—when it got hard enough, it was considered toast.

At the end of the counter, Jonny frowned at a pair of empty pans. They were supposed to contain margarine, but both had been scraped clean. He knew that it would just make the bread harder to get down, an expected consequence of getting to chow late.

Moving out among the crowded tables, Jonny made his way toward one that was four rows in and against the north wall. Claude was there already. Joining his friend, Jonny sat in his usual seat—his back to the wall. A second later, Seth sat down across from him, in the seat they had given him when he showed up at the prison.

"What's up, bro?" Jonny directed the question to Claude, who he could tell had something he wanted to tell him.

"Someone's going to get hit."

"Who?"

"Dino."

Jonny glanced at a prisoner seated twenty feet away at one of the skinhead tables. "You'd think what they did to Ernie would be enough," he said.

Jonny did not like thinking about what had happened to Ernie. He had been doused with gasoline and burned in his cell only three days prior. Until the attack, he had led this group of skinheads and Dino was his lieutenant. The sound still haunted Jonny—the sound of Ernie screaming while he was on fire—he felt sick thinking about it. Ernie had screamed for as long as he was able. He may have had his problems, Jonny thought, but he didn't deserve what had been done to him. No one did.

Incredibly, Ernie was still alive when guards dragged him, still smoldering, out of his cell. Although no one there knew if he still was. He had been burned over 85 percent of his body, most severely on his head and hands. His lips were gone and so were his eyelids and eyes. He'd held onto the bars of his cell while he burned. When guards extinguished him and pried him away from them, several of his fingers had broken off.

"If he had any sense, he'd know it's coming," Jonny said. Claude shrugged, displaying his indifference.

Everyone knew that the order had come into the prison to hit a black prisoner—one who had arrived recently after being convicted of killing a young white guy during a drunken street riot in Seattle. Not seeing the order through is what earned Ernie his fate. And in the mind of whoever it was calling the shot, Jonny knew Dino was seen as no less deserving of being dealt with.

Jonny looked at Seth and saw that he had already eaten nearly everything on his tray. The youngster always seemed like he was starving. Gathering up some of the sponge-like egg material on his own plastic spoon, Jonny began to eat.

"Here." Claude pushed his tray toward him. It had been cleaned of food, but there was still a bit of margarine in the corner compartment.

"Thanks."

That was just like Claude, Jonny thought, always looking out for his friends. They had first met at the

Bay, which was where Claude had begun his stretch. They both had. He had been in for nearly as long as Jonny too, which meant he had about 90 years left to do. Cops had caught him in a burglary and he decided to shoot at them in order to try to get away. He didn't hit any of them, but that didn't matter. They *broke him off* anyway. Four cops, four counts of first-degree assault running wild: twenty-five years on each.

But knowing why Claude was in prison only made Jonny respect him more. He didn't give a shit what the cops, the court, or anyone else thought. He knew Claude was a good dude.

"You guys want coffee?" Seth asked, standing up suddenly.

Claude shook his head as he continued to watch the skinhead tables. Anyone watching him would not realize that was what he was doing.

Jonny shook his head too. He didn't drink the coffee in the Chowhall, and for good reason. He had seen it made in the back of the kitchen and knew that it wasn't actually coffee. The fact that it was dark and warm was about the only thing it had in common with real coffee.

"He's going to turn out all right," Claude remarked after Seth left the table.

"Maybe," Jonny said, raising a slice of bread to his mouth. He spotted the duck he had seen earlier in the showers.

"Look..." Jonny nudged Claude with his elbow and nodded toward the duck, who was wandering between tables, a distressed expression on his face. He was looking for a place to sit. He tried to sit down at a table of older convicts that had an open seat, but they chased him away quickly with sharp words and menacing glares.

"He ain't going to make it," Jonny remarked. "I saw him down in the showers this morning trying to shower on the *toad* side."

"He's a *rapo*," Claude informed him matter-of-fact-ly. Jonny's eyes widened. "There's a guy here from his county. Says he's in on a rape beef."

"What's he still doing out here?" Jonny asked, a trace of incredulity in his voice.

"Riff Raff's going to hook him up."

"Oh-h-h." Jonny raised his eyebrows and nodded in sudden comprehension.

The duck gave up trying to find a seat and began eating what he could off of his tray while he stood in an aisle.

Claude nudged Jonny's arm and redirected his attention toward the skinhead tables. A stocky, young skinhead stood up and cast a telltale glance at Dino's back two tables away. Seth returned and sat down, but Jonny and Claude's attention remained fixed on the skinhead. He began moving in Dino's direction. This was it, Jonny thought. No question about it now.

As the skinhead approached his target, the noise level in their section of the Chowhall dropped perceptibly. Talking with others at his table, Dino missed the cue, which is the only thing that might have given him a fighting chance, if he had any at all.

Jonny looked over at the line of guards just inside the Chowhall entrance and realized that they were watching too. Did they know? Obviously they did. Nothing surprised him anymore about what the guards knew.

Jonny turned in time to see the skinhead strike Dino from behind with a heavy, clubbing blow to the base of the skull. He put everything into it and, as a result, Dino crumpled. The sound of his limp body striking the greasy tile floor in the suddenly silent Chowhall seemed loud. Everyone was watching now.

The skinhead set to work kicking and stomping Dino. Another jumped up and joined the attack, this one from the same table where Dino had been sitting. They concentrated their efforts on their victim's head, kicking him full-force in his blood-covered face and causing his neck to snap back and forth violently.

"Break it up! Break it up!"

Prisoners dropped to the floor everywhere, prodded by the guards on the balcony, who were yelling and waving their shotguns. Jonny, Seth, and Claude were no exception. They crouched down quickly beside their table as guards rushed in through the front doors, adding themselves to those that were already there. A mass of blue started toward the altercation.

"Stop fighting! Break it up!" The guards on the balcony yelled again.

The two attackers changed tactics. They dropped down over the body—one of them straddling Dino's chest—and went to work on his face with their fists, burying it beneath a barrage of punishing blows. Blood flew upward in dark splashes that Jonny could see even from where he was.

When guards got to them, they gained control quickly. Half a dozen grabbed hold of each attacker and dragged them away from the body, pinning them to the floor a short distance away.

Raising his head a bit in order to get a better view of what was going on, Jonny spotted Lt. Todd entering the Chowhall. He felt the familiar sensation of his hatred for him rise up immediately. Fixing his attention on the lieutenant's black leather eye patch as he approached, it struck Jonny that there was no possibility that this man could ever be mistaken for anything other than what he was. If a movie were ever made about a prison with a really evil lieutenant, Jonny knew this would be the man they would want to play the role. He certainly wouldn't have to rehearse his part.

When he reached them, Lt. Todd looked down at the two prisoners who were laid out on their bellies with their hands cuffed behind their backs and guards sitting or kneeling on them to ensure they weren't able to get up. He turned his attention to the one who had initiated the attack.

"Why'd you make this mess in my Chowhall?"

There was no response and, without blinking or altering his expression, the lieutenant kicked the prisoner in the face. The kick didn't look hard but, Jonny knew that with a steel-toed boot, it didn't need to be. It had been one just like it, six years earlier, that had given him the jagged scar on his own lip and knocked out his front tooth.

"You're a COWARD, Todd!"

Lt. Todd's head spun in the direction the shouted remark had come from, but it was impossible for him to pinpoint. There were too many prisoners in too large a space. Turning back to the prisoner in front of him, he kicked him again. This time harder.

"Get down!"

One of the guards on the balcony bellowed as both shotguns were brought to bear on a prisoner that had begun to rise in response to the last kick. Jonny saw that he was a skinhead too.

Glaring hate, the prisoner sank down again slowly. He was lucky to have gotten a warning, and everyone in the Chowhall knew it.

Lt. Todd looked around at the hundreds of prisoners laid out on the floor, surveying them in silence for a long moment. Finally, he broke the silence in a voice that reflected his disgust.

"Get 'em out of here."

The guards responded immediately, pulling the two skinheads to their feet and lifting their cuffed wrists high behind their backs, forcing them to stoop forward and look down at the ground as they were marched away. Blood ran from the nostrils of the one who had been kicked. It could have been worse, Jonny thought, unconsciously biting the twisted scar tissue that ran through his lip.

The guards ratcheted handcuffs onto Dino too, even though he was still out cold. Four of them lifted him from the floor like baggage, one on each ankle and one on each elbow.

"Jesus," Seth murmured, as Dino's head fell forward and they caught sight of his face. He was no longer recognizable—his visage, a torn and bloody impostor, hideous in its ruin and streaming an unbroken trail of blood as he was taken away. Lt. Todd and the remaining guards followed him out.

When they were gone, the guards on the balcony lowered their shotguns and prisoners pushed themselves up off the floor. Sitting back down at their tables, the activity and noise level inside the Chowhall resumed.

"You bring any smokes?" Claude asked, sounding hopeful.

Reaching into the pocket of his coat, Jonny took out a small foil pouch and set it on the table in front of him. Unfolding the top, he removed a sheaf of cigarette papers and separated three from the others. Keeping one for himself, he passed one to Claude and the other to Seth.

Jonny glanced up at the balcony to make sure the guards weren't watching. There was a rule against rolling cigarettes in the Chowhall. If the guards saw them, they would take his tobacco on the way out.

Reaching into the pouch, Jonny took out a pinch of shredded leaf and set it in the center of the paper that he had deftly perched between the fingers of his left hand. Distributing the tobacco evenly, he was careful not to lose any. Folding the paper over and in on itself, he began to work it back and forth between his thumbs and forefingers, then to roll it. Finally, he brought the paper up and traced the tip of his tongue lightly across the length of its unfastened edge. Rolling his thumbs forward the last fraction of an inch, he sealed it.

Jonny surveyed his creation for a moment with a critical eye, then tucked it into the fold of his stocking cap and returned the pouch of tobacco to his pocket. Seeing the cigarette Seth had rolled, he laughed. It bulged ridiculously in the middle and tapered to near nothing at the ends. The young prisoner would get better, Jonny thought, but from the looks of it, it would take awhile.

The three of them got up and left the table together. At the door, guards were selecting prisoners at random to pat-search from the line of people leaving. Joining the line, Jonny banged his tray against the inside of a slop barrel, despite the fact that nothing remained on it, and slid it through a wide slot in the wall. Turning toward the exit, he began to wipe his hands together as though something from the slop barrel had gotten on them. Passing by the guards, he wiped them on his pants as if he were trying to get it off.

Outside, Jonny paused to strike a match and touch it to the end of his cigarette. He handed what remained of the book to Claude who had walked out behind him.

"Where's Seth?"

"They pulled him over," Claude said, returning the matches once his cigarette was lit. Jonny breathed in slowly, attempting to mitigate the sting of the frozen air in his nostrils. "It's fucking cold," Claude complained, his voice already shivery. He flipped up the frayed collar of his state-issue coat and buried his hands in its pockets. "It couldn't be any worse if they sent us to Siberia."

Jonny laughed. "You going to work?"

"Yeah."

They shook hands briefly before turning and heading in opposite directions. Jonny did not envy his friend, who was on the garbage crew and would be working outside all day. Sometimes Claude's job had benefits, but on days like this, Jonny couldn't think of a single one.

Despite the cold, Jonny walked slowly. He always took his time walking back from chow. The way he saw it, there was no use in hurrying. For what? To get back to his cell and get locked in?

As he brought the cigarette to his lips, Jonny's hand

rubbed against his stubbled jaw. It had been awhile since he shaved. Not that it mattered. It just reminded him of when they first sent him to prison. He had not been able to grow facial hair then. It seemed like a lifetime ago.

He looked across the frozen courtyard at the massive gray wall that surrounded the prison and saw a guard standing on the catwalk of a gun tower. The mesh enclosing the catwalk had grown a furry rime of hoarfrost, and beneath it hung an impressive array of icicles. They reminded Jonny of what a set of perfect dinosaur teeth might look like on a gray stone monster. The guard was bundled against the cold and cradled a rifle. His breath, a frozen plume trailing away from an indistinguishable face. For a moment, Jonny wondered what he himself might look like through the guard's eyes.

"Jonny! Wait up!"

Jonny slowed his pace even further, but he didn't come to a complete stop. He didn't want to provoke the guard in the tower. That could mean trouble.

He and Seth returned to the cell-house together. When they reached their cell, Jonny saw that inside a sheet had been hung between the ends of the bunks, closing off the back. He swung the sign out and, a second later, the cell door shimmied in its frame and rolled open. Folding the sign back against the bars, he and Seth entered and unwittingly stepped into the unseen embrace of a malodorous assault.

"Uuughh! Flush it, Corey! You're killing us!"

The toilet flushed and the sound of Corey's voice came to them from behind the curtain. "Sorry."

Jonny noticed the look of revulsion on Seth's face and checked the urge to laugh. "You better hurry, I think Seth's going to puke."

"C'mon, it ain't that bad," Corey said, sounding genuinely hurt.

Pressing his stocking cap to his nose, Seth rolled his eyes. Using the end of his footlocker for a step, he leapt onto his bunk and laid down keeping the cap pressed to his face.

Jonny stepped up onto his own footlocker and set to work making his bunk. He always waited until after he returned from breakfast to do this because Matt was gone to work by this time and they would not be in each other's way. Prisoners who worked in the metal plant did not wait for the regular work call like everyone else. The industry bosses wanted them at their work stations sooner. Jonny supposed that was so the state could get more license plates out of them.

The toilet flushed again, and Corey stood up behind the sheet. At 6'4," 320 pounds, he was a massive prisoner whose arms and torso were covered in prison ink. As he took down the sheet and folded it, Jonny' s eyes were drawn (as they often were) to the large Old English letters across the back of his cellie's shoulders: "METH 'TIL DEATH." Beneath the words was a wicked-looking skull sitting atop a mountain of bones. It was very good work.

Finishing with the bunk, Jonny sat on the end of his footlocker and began to untie his boots while Corey ran water over his hands at the sink. He remembered the first time he had met his cellie. It had been Corey's first stretch in prison, when he was in on a burglary. He had been out since then but had returned with a fresh thirty-year sentence that, like nearly everything else bad that happened to him, he was somehow able to take in stride.

Corey had earned his latest trip to prison for running a meth lab. The state buried him under a mountain of charges: multiple counts of manufacture and sale of methamphetamine, with a firearm enhancement on each count, and an additional enhancement for having his lab within a thousand yards of a school bus stop. Even though the judge gave him the low end of the mandatory sentence, he never had a chance.

Jonny was glad that he and Corey were cellies

though. Under any other circumstance, he would not choose to live with anyone over 200 pounds because the cells there just were not big enough for it. But to Jonny Corey was worth making an exception for because he was the most successful person he had ever known. Corey had learned to make meth from an older con while he was in on his first stretch. And when he got out he had done well applying the newly acquired skill. He accrued a small house on five acres, a truck only a couple of years old, and a motorcycle, all within a relatively short time. It was hard for Jonny to imagine a person owning all those things, and he might not even have believed it if it were not for the pictures that his cellie kept in an overfilled album in his footlocker. In fact, the album had become Corey's most valued possession—the actual property the photos were of long since seized under civil forfeiture laws and sold at auction by the county.

Removing his boots, Jonny stepped back up onto the footlocker and was gathering himself to make the leap for the top bunk when Corey's voice stopped him.

"Will you *keep point* while I get the gun out?"

"Sure."

Jonny went to the bars at the front of the cell and reached a hand up to the steel runner above the door. His fingers slipped inside and he felt around for a moment. When his hand came back down, it contained a small piece of broken mirror. Extending his hand out through the bars, Jonny turned the mirror fragment so that he had a view down the tier in its reflection. He nodded to Corey who turned and went to work on the electrical outlet set high in the center of the wall at the back of the cell.

"Dino got beat down this morning," Jonny said, not taking his eyes off the tier.

"Well, maybe that's the end of it," Corey remarked, as he removed the outlet cover. "We shouldn't be taking each other out, it only makes us white motherfuckers weaker. It's what the other races want us to do."

Jonny wasn't sure that was true, but he saw no point in arguing, so he remained silent. Digging his fingers in behind a mass of wiring, Corey pulled out a package wrapped in plastic, then reset the plate over the outlet.

"Okay."

Jonny returned the mirror fragment to its hiding place and joined his cellie in the back of the cell, where he sat on a stool in front of a small wood table abutting the end of his bunk. Corey dwarfed the table and stool, but that was the effect he had on most things. Jonny watched as he unwrapped the package that contained his prison-made tattoo gun, needles fashioned from a sharpened guitar string, and ink.

This was another thing Jonny liked about Corey. He was a master of hustle inside of prison. And slinging ink was one of his hustles. He was good at it, putting out some of the best work in the joint.

"You need any help?"

"Nah." Corey shook his head. "Everything's already set and ready to roll."

Jonny frowned, feeling a trace of disappointment. He liked to help when it came to tattooing and wished that he was able to pick up the skill. Corey had spent quite a bit of time trying to teach him, but Jonny found it hard enough to draw on a piece of paper. Learning to scratch a picture into someone's flesh with a needle he knew would take a lot more practice. He wondered if Corey had given up trying to teach him.

"I got a couple of papers for Hawk and Mack," Corey said, not looking up as he assembled the gun. "You think you can get them over to them?"

Jonny shrugged. "Sure."

Corey nodded toward two tiny, plastic-wrapped packages on the table. Jonny scooped them up and went to his bunk.

These "papers" (each the size of a match head) were actually pieces of black tar heroin, which Corey sometimes received as payment for tattoo work. Jonny didn't mind transporting and delivering them because of the prosperity it brought to their cell. They weren't rich, but he knew that if it was not for what Corey hustled, they would do a lot worse than they did. Delivering this stuff allowed Jonny to feel like he was at least a part of that.

Jonny lay on his bunk for less than a minute when the cellblock loudspeakers crackled to life. "Work call! Eight o' clock work call!"

The cell door opened at the same time as the one hundred and one others inside the cell-house. The metal clanging clamor was deafening.

Jonny popped the two plastic-covered packages into his mouth, tucking them behind his gums before jumping down and giving the sleeping Seth a shove.

"C'mon, it's work call."

Grabbing his boots, he slipped out the door and sat down on the tier to put them on. A moment later, a groggy, grumbling Seth made it out behind him just as the door was slamming closed.

They left the tier together and descended the stairs, crowding into the front end of the cell-house with everyone else leaving for work. Traffic was backed up in front of the metal detector because prisoners were arriving faster than they were able to pass through.

Jonny waited, noticing that the three guards posted beside the detector weren't paying attention to the prisoners streaming past. They were talking to Daugherty, the chief cell-house porter. Jonny's jaw tightened when he saw him. He couldn't stand the sight of the fat, bald-headed rat, who he knew was willing to sell out his fellow prisoners for whatever it was the guards gave him to do it. Maybe even for nothing at all. Something bad was going to happen to him, Jonny thought. It always did to people like that in prison.

Pouring out of the cell-house with the rest of the work crowd, the cold air struck Jonny anew, biting into his ears and freezing his nostrils as he fumbled to put on his stocking cap. Claude was right. It was cold—the kind of cold that, no matter how much you believed you were prepared for it, it always caught you off guard, snatching your breath and piercing your state-issue clothing with its wintry breath.

To Jonny's left, huddled in a group near the back door of the kitchen, were two dozen prisoners wearing white coveralls beneath their coats. Jonny was relieved to see them. He had not been sure if they would be out there on break or not. Telling Seth that he would catch up to him at the gate, Jonny veered out of the line of prisoners going to work and headed toward them. Seeing him approach, one of them separated himself from the group.

"Hey Hawk," Jonny greeted the older man as he drew close. "I hope that wasn't you who made that crap they dished out for breakfast."

Hawk chuckled. "Don't blame me, Jonny. I can only work with what they give me." Jonny shook hands with the grizzled cook. He wondered why the older prisoner's coveralls had looked so white from a distance when, up close, he could see they were anything but that. In fact, he saw that all of the workers were wearing filthy, stain-covered coveralls. Hawk's words played over in his mind—that he could only work with what he was given. Jonny supposed that went for the coveralls as well.

"Matt wants to catch up with you in the Yard tonight. You going out?" As Jonny asked the question, he tried to assess how closely they were being observed by the other workers. He knew that was one of the unavoidable things about prison, that there were always eyes watching. It was a delusion to believe you could actually do something without being seen. The trick, of course, wasn't not to do what you needed to do—it was to do it in a way that made whoever was observing believe what they were seeing was something other than what it was.

"I'll be out," Hawk said. "Let him know I'll be there."

Jonny nodded, lifting a hand to his face and rubbing his stubbled upper lip with his thumb and forefinger as though trying to smooth down a mustache. Lowering his hand, he returned it to his coat pocket, readjusting the tiny plastic-wrapped lump he had slipped out from between his lips. He tucked it between his second and third fingers.

"Thank you, Jonny," Hawk said, genuinely grateful in the way only a dope fiend can be. He shook Jonny's hand and took possession of the packet.

Jonny made his way carefully over the ice-covered concrete of the courtyard, chasing the last of the workers leaving the cell-house. When he reached the Chowhall, he turned onto the street that ran down the center of the prison. It was lined closely by buildings on either side, all of them composed of the same old turn-of-the-century brickwork as the cell-house. Ahead, a large backup of prisoners had formed in front of a steel roll-up gate that spanned the street from one side to the other.

This was just like them to pick a cold ass day like it was to close the gate, Jonny thought. Instead of letting prisoners pass through and go to their workplaces unmolested, guards were opening a smaller sliding-type security door off to the side and allowing only a dozen prisoners at a time to crowd their way into a small holding area where they were searched before being allowed to proceed. Jonny could see that it was going to take a long time for them to work their way through everyone. He caught sight of Seth who stood taller than the other prisoners around him. The youngster was near the door, in the densest part of the crowd. Shouting to get his attention, Jonny began to make his way through the throng as diplomatically as he could, earning a number of looks in the process. As he drew near, the security door opened and prisoners again began to spill through into the holding area. He moved with the surge, making it to the doorway just as it began to close. Stepping through quickly, he allowed enough space for another prisoner to squeeze in behind him.

That was as close as Jonny liked to cut it. At least, as close as he was comfortable with since they had thrown him in the Hole for merely brushing against the side of the door while it was closing. He had decided then that starving for thirty days was not worth trying to get to work a little earlier.

Seth had held back in the crowd and now stood beside Jonny. Ahead of them, guards pat-searched prisoners four at a time while a sergeant checked names and work crews off a list. Lt. Todd stood behind the guards, which only caused them to take more time and search more thoroughly than they would if he was not there.

Jonny realized they were checking clothes. Anyone wearing a clothing item without their number stamped on it, or with one that was not their own, was being ordered to take it off and toss it onto a growing pile. Jonny knew because of how cold it was that many prisoners were wearing at least one thing that was not theirs. After all, if your cellie worked in the warm kitchen all day and you had to work outside, what was wrong with borrowing his sweatshirt or stocking cap in order to keep yourself from freezing? Jonny noted that the guards were wearing good quality cold weather gear that had been furnished for them by the state. It only made it more ridiculous that they were taking clothes from people dressed as shabbily as they were.

Jonny thought about Claude and wondered if the sweatshirt his friend wore at breakfast was in the pile. He had no doubt that it was because—like Jonny—he did not have anyone in the *freeworld* to send him clothes.

The searching came to a halt when an older, Asian-looking prisoner began to argue with the guards about the thermal underwear they had ordered him to take off. Lt. Todd stepped forward and both guards and prisoner fell silent. Jonny knew what would happen next, the outcome of the scene as easy to predict as the future of someone lying down on railroad tracks in front of an oncoming train.

"Lock his ass up," Lt. Todd growled, his single eye somehow more menacing than two would have been.

Guards grabbed the prisoner and put handcuffs on him. Holding the old man firmly by his arms, two of them ushered him quickly through a side door that everyone knew led to the Hole.

When it was Jonny's turn to be searched, he began to cough. It came over him unexpectedly, and he bent forward, hacking forcefully into his hand. It was not intentional this time and he struggled to bring it under control. The guard closest to him looked irritated.

Stepping forward and turning his back to the guard, Jonny opened his coat and removed his hat. He held his arms straight out from his sides as the guard began a heavy-handed search. Jonny felt himself bristle. He hated when they touched him. It was a sobering reminder that he was in control of nothing. As the hands beat their way down his sides, he heard the guard to his left snap at Seth.

"Your ID belongs on the left side!"

The guard was referring to the green ID card prisoners were required to keep clipped to the left, uppermost portion of their clothing. For some reason, Seth had fallen into the habit of clipping it on his right side, which Jonny didn't understand because it only invited trouble. He wondered if the youngster knew the difference.

The guard behind Jonny flipped up the back of his coat to check the number stamped in it. Jonny was not worried because everything he was wearing belonged to the state and had been issued to him. It was thin, poor quality clothing that offered little protection from the cold, but he was used to it. The guard snatched the stocking cap from his hand and shook it briefly before handing it back.

"Whose boots are those?"

"They're mine," Jonny answered, not allowing a second of pause between the question and his response.

Actually, they were not his and, technically, he was not supposed to have them. However, he balked at the thought of giving them up. They were not good boots by freeworld standards, but they were a thousand times better than the vinyl and plastic shoes most of the rest of the population wore. His crew leader, Anton, had paid off the Clothing Room clerk for them, and they had since become Jonny's most valued possession.

"You got a receipt?" The guard pressed him, knowing full well that even if the boots were Jonny's, he would not carry a receipt around for them.

"Mr. Marks issued them to me."

Jonny's response caused the guard to pause. Department heads could order boots for their workers but, since it required a mountain of paperwork, it was a rare prisoner who got them—at least, through legitimate channels.

"You're on the janitor crew?"

Jonny nodded.

"So, when I call Marks, he's going to tell me that he issued those to you?"

"Yeah," Jonny said, realizing that he was in the clear. The guard had not ordered him to take off the boots and now it did not seem likely that he would. Besides, Jonny thought, the only reason he was giving him trouble was because Lt. Todd was there. By the time the guard finished with all the pat-searches he had left to do, it was not likely that he would remember or even care enough to call Mr. Marks and check out his story.

Jonny walked away without waiting to be dismissed and joined the others who had been searched. A large sliding door at the opposite end of the holding area opened and they poured out. They were now on the other side of the roll-up gate.

"I hate that shit," Seth remarked when they were on

their way again.

Jonny did not respond. Fact was, he didn't like it either, but he knew it didn't do any good to wallow in what he felt about it. Forget it and move on. The ability to do that was a necessary skill in that place.

He and Seth made their way across the prison, which was like a city all to itself. Its cracked and potholed streets were lined with old buildings that crowded in on each other from either side.

Rounding a corner, Jonny swore under his breath when he saw Anton standing in front of a two-story building that looked even older than the others around it. The mortar between its weathered bricks had long since begun to crumble and fall out. The first floor housed their shop, Custodial Services, and the fact that their crew leader was outside meant that Mr. Marks was not there yet. They would have to wait outside in the cold until he arrived to let them in.

"Good morning," Anton greeted them.

Jonny and Seth acknowledged him in turn, then looked glumly in the direction of the locked shop door.

"Where's Mr. Marks?" Jonny asked.

Anton shrugged, not bothering to respond to the obvious.

Jonny zipped his coat as far as it would go and pushed his cap down lower on his brow. Walking over to a steel cart parked next to the shop door, he sat down.

"I'll go see if I can find him," Anton said, pushing his hands deeper into the pockets of his coat. "He's probably out front somewhere and needs someone to remind him where he works."

As Anton disappeared down the street, Seth sat down beside Jonny on the cart. "He ain't coming back."

Jonny chuckled as he tucked his chin behind the raised collar of his coat, trying to retain as much warmth as possible.

"You blame him?"

Seth shook his head. The truth was he respected

and looked up to Anton. He and Jonny both did. Anton was a good crew leader and a veteran convict who was ten years older than Jonny and had been in twice as long. The way Jonny saw it, anyone who had been in twenty years and held themselves together as well as Anton deserved respect. That much time was a hell of a thing, although that was not what intrigued Jonny most about their crew leader. What he found most interesting about Anton—even to the point of reverence—was that he was the most influential and luck-blessed person Jonny had ever known. He seemed encircled with an aura that attracted others to him and caused things to go his way. Even looking at him was somehow magnetizing. He was tall with long blond hair that he kept tied back tightly and he had the carriage and build of a well-conditioned athlete. Jonny often thought he looked more like an actor playing the part of someone in that place, instead of what he actually was. He wished that he could be more like him.

Taking his hands out of his pockets and cupping them to his mouth, Jonny blew into them in an attempt to warm his frozen fingers. On the street he saw an old man he recognized from one of the other cell-houses. Every few yards the old prisoner bent down to pick something up and Jonny realized he was *snipe hunting*. Looking toward the nearest gun tower, Jonny wondered for a moment if the guard inside would yell at him, but he did not come out. It was going to take more than an old snipe hunter to get him outside in this cold.

A door at the top of a staircase on a nearby building opened and two prisoners stepped out. Seeing Jonny, they started down the stairs.

Jonny stood up, eliciting a questioning look from Seth. "I'll be back." The young prisoner rolled his eyes and shook his head.

"No, really. I just gotta talk with Mack for a minute. I wouldn't leave you out here to freeze by yourself."

As he crossed the street, Jonny noted that it felt better to be up and moving. He was still freezing, but at least he wasn't sitting still doing it. The double doors on the front of the building he was approaching swung open and three prisoners exited, joining Mack and the prisoner that was with him at the bottom of the stairs. This caused Jonny to frown, as he realized it would not be as easy as he had hoped. He spit the tiny package of heroin into his hand before any of the three saw him.

"Jonny!" Mack greeted him warmly. The graying older convict was rolling a cigarette and offered his pouch.

Jonny noted that the others, after giving him no more than a glance, returned their attention to the conversation they were involved in between each other. That is, except for Tony who continued to watch him. Jonny accepted the pouch Mack offered but refrained from making the move.

Pinching a tuft of loose tobacco from the end of the cigarette he had just rolled, Mack passed it to Tony who, since losing the fingers on his right hand, was no longer able to roll for himself. Striking a match, Mack held it out to him, touching its flame to the end of the cigarette while Tony inhaled. Tony's eyes remained fixed on Jonny.

As far as Jonny knew, chasing dope had always been what was most important to Tony—even though, since losing his job at the metal plant, he never had anything to offer in exchange for it. He had been fired for getting his fingers cut off. It did not seem fair to Jonny that they would fire a guy for that. On the other hand, if a prisoner no longer had enough fingers to do the job, he supposed the plant manager didn't have a choice.

Jonny averted his eyes from Tony's hand. He didn't like looking at it. Tony still had a thumb, but the rest of the fingers had been sheared off at their base. He didn't even have stubs left.

With his own unfeeling fingers, Jonny pushed a clump of dry leaf into the center of a rolling paper. A breeze licked at it, and he turned in order to keep it from whisking the tobacco away. Blocking Tony's line of sight with his back, he dropped the heroin into the pouch. Turning again, he licked the edge of the rolling paper and pressed it down. Then, holding the cigarette aloft, he surveyed his work, as was his habit. It looked nearly as bad as one of Seth's, but it was the best he could do with hands that no longer felt like they were his own.

"Thanks," Jonny said, handing the tobacco back to Mack. "You're a lifesaver."

Tony's eyes remained on the pouch as it exchanged hands and Jonny wondered if he knew. Dope fiend intuition was a motherfucker.

"Jonny."

Jonny had already turned to leave when one of the other prisoners—a short, stocky Chicano he knew was named Chivo—hailed him. The prisoner approached and extended his hand.

"What's up, Jonny? How's it going?"

Jonny shook the Chicano's hand and nodded. The prisoner did not know him well enough for small talk. He wanted something and Jonny waited to hear what it was.

"You guys have any more stones in your shop?"

Jonny eyed the Chicano warily. The stones he was referring to were small blocks of pumice used to clean tile grout—although, in prison they were more often used to sharpen shanks. Jonny's mind went to work on the possible implications.

"No. We're out," Jonny answered, after a pause. Reading his hesitation, the Chicano tried again.

"It's for the *mayates*, Jonny. We need to hit them hard this time...so maybe it won't have to be done again for a long time.

Jonny nodded thoughtfully—not that he was agreeing to anything, only that he was listening.

"You guys have coffee over there?"

The Chicano knew it was likely Jonny's crew didn't.

They did not have access to it like he did, because he worked in the gym where coffee was furnished by the prison for the guards. Real coffee.

Jonny's wariness evaporated. "You going to be in the gym all morning?" The Chicano nodded.

"I'll be over," Jonny said, taking his hand out of his pocket in order to shake and lock in the agreement.

As Jonny drew near, he saw Seth still seated on the cart in front of their shop, although something seemed not quite right about him. Reaching him, Jonny realized that the young prisoner was asleep. Resting with his back against the worn brick of the building, he was snoring softly.

"Incredible," Jonny said, speaking to himself as he contemplated the twin rivulets of frozen mucus that had formed beneath the young prisoner's nostrils. The kid could sleep anywhere. Jonny checked the urge to wake him and sat down quietly on the cart beside him instead.

Jonny thought about the cigarette tucked in his cap, the one he had rolled out of Mack's tobacco. He decided against it. His hands were too cold. He was not going to take them out of his pockets again for anything.

Jonny heard the clatter of the steel roll-up gate being opened down the street. He knew that it meant that all prisoners had made it through the search enclosure. A minute later, a half dozen guards moved along the street laughing and joking with each other. They lacked the sense of haste that prisoners wearing state-issue clothing felt on days as cold as this. Jonny remained still, hoping that they did not notice him or Seth. Freezing like this was bad enough. He did not want to have to deal with them on top of it.

When the guards passed, Jonny leaned back against the building and tried to relax. His mother had told him once that if a person relaxed when they were cold, they would stop shivering. He tried to do it. A scratching sound came from around the corner of the building and, a moment later, its source shuffled into view carrying the tools of his trade: a small broom and a long-handled dustpan. Jonny watched the breezeway porter work down the street. Remembering the old man who had passed by earlier, he doubted there were many butts left to sweep up. No fresh ones anyway.

Jonny gave up the effort to relax and tightened his muscles, trying to steel himself against the trembling that had taken him over. As soon as he let up, he began to shake again. This time it was worse, as though his body were retaliating against his attempt to control it. It simply was not possible to relax in this kind of cold, he realized.

The memory of his mother's advice brought her image strongly into Jonny's mind. He admonished himself for not writing to her more often. His mother had moved to California six years earlier with his younger sister. It had not really changed anything between them though. Even while she lived in Seattle she had not been able to visit him there. Nearly 500 miles and a mountain range separated them. Even if she could have afforded to take the time off work, it was not likely that her old Buick could have survived the trip.

Jonny wondered what his sister looked like. She was twelve when they locked him up—a dark-haired little girl in grade school. He realized that she would be twenty-two now, but he could not churn up a picture for that inside himself. The last time he saw her had been at the hospital, shortly before they transferred him to the jail. She cried then. And that is how he remembered her—her dark hair in braids and tears streaming down her cheeks.

Nearly a year had passed since the last letter he had received from his mother, but he believed another would arrive soon because it was close to Christmas. She wrote to him every year around this time. And she always enclosed a twenty-dollar money order in her letter. Jonny had never told her that the state took 85 percent (for restitution and "Cost of Incarceration" fee) because he did not want her to feel like she was not able to help him.

It surprised Jonny that his mother's letters made it to him because she did not address them correctly or put his prison number on them. Written on the outside of each envelope in her meticulously ornate hand, she would write:

Jonny Anderson

Walla Walla Prison

He had sent her his number and correct address a number of times. Even though he knew why she did not use it:

#605666

Washington State Penitentiary

1313 North 13th St.

His mother went to church and, well, if Satan himself had an address, Jonny was sure it would be close to his.

Jonny knew that it was his own fault that writing to his mother had become harder for him, because he had lied to her from the start. He felt bad about doing it, but there was no way he was going to tell her what it was really like there. He had told her that he was in auto mechanics school, which was what he had always wanted to do. But there was no school for that inside the prison. There was not a school for anything there anymore. Education inside prison had long since been gutted by state officials because, as they said, they did not believe it was right to reward people for committing crime.

Jonny dug his elbow into Seth's side. "Here they come."

Jonny and Seth got stiffly to their feet as Mr. Marks approached with Kevin, a middle-aged black prisoner who was the other member of their four-man work crew.

"Hope you two haven't been out here long," Mr. Marks said as he stepped in front of the shop door and flipped through keys on his overfilled ring.

Jonny did not say anything. His face was frozen and he was unsure of his ability to enunciate.

When the custodial supervisor settled on the correct key, he inserted it in the door's lock and worked it back and forth several times, simultaneously pulling on the door's handle. After a few tugs, the door opened.

The shop was not as warm as the cell-house, although heat from the steamlines in the basement made it a considerable improvement over being outside. There was also a small space heater that Jonny wasted no time in switching on. They had stolen it from the guard station in Six Wing during the summer so that it would not immediately be missed.

In keeping with his routine, Mr. Marks went to his office and shut the door. Jonny remembered that he had meant to say something to him about the boots.

Kevin pushed a wet-vac out to the center of the shop floor and began to inspect it. Jonny knew that he was from Seattle too, and had been in the Marines during the Iraq war. Over the time they had worked together, Jonny had come to respect him.

"Where are we going?" Jonny tested the words, still not certain they would come out right. They did.

"The showers flooded in Six Wing," Kevin said as he inspected the vacuum's filter. "Anton's already over there."

Jonny left his place near the heater before he had a chance to benefit from it and went to the far end of the shop. He began pulling mop heads from a barrel. Seth moved to the spot Jonny had ceded.

"Grab the floor squeegees out of the back," Jonny told the younger prisoner as he dropped an armload of mop heads into a plastic bucket.

Jonny was weighing whether or not to knock on Marks's door and ask him for one of the pumice stones he kept in the locked cabinet behind his desk, when he heard Seth cry out. He and Kevin found him in the storeroom behind their shop, which, except for a small section they used to store supplies, was a graveyard of broken and no-longer-used equipment from around the prison. In the dull luminescence cast by the flickering fluorescent light, Jonny saw what had the young prisoner's attention. A mouse struggled at his feet. Half of the tiny animal was caught in the sticky resin on a small plastic plate designed specifically for what it had done.

Jonny swore under his breath. He thought he had cleared the shop of all the traps the guard who had been through a week earlier had dispensed.

This was the type of trap used at the prison. A mouse need only touch it to be caught. And the more the creature struggled to free itself, the more deeply it would become mired. Jonny hated seeing mice in these traps because there was nothing that could be done for them. It was why he threw them away whenever he found them.

Seth squatted down beside the mouse and studied him, an expression of concern on his face. Jonny felt something nudge his arm and he turned to see Kevin holding a dustpan out to him. He had worked with the ex-Marine long enough to know why he was giving it to him. As unlikely as it might seem, he was afraid of mice.

The mouse began to move its limbs frantically as Jonny moved in with the dustpan. Its body remained fixed in the resin.

"What are you doing?" Seth said, alarmed.

"We can't leave him like this," Jonny told him. "It's best if we just get it over with."

"We can save him."

Kevin groaned in disgust at the young prisoner's suggestion. "Jesus Christ."

"I don't think there's anything we can do for him," Jonny said. "If you try to pull him out, it'll tear the skin off him."

"We can figure out a way to do it," Seth insisted, looking up from where he crouched over the mouse.

"He's not all the way in the stuff, it's only got half of him. Maybe if we warm it up a little, we can get him out."

"We don't have time," Jonny told him. "We're supposed to be in Six Wing." Seth did not move.

Jonny looked down at the mouse still struggling to free itself. The tiny animal stopped moving suddenly and looked up at him. Jonny imagined that he could see resignation in its eyes.

"Fuck." Jonny flung the dustpan away. Grabbing a rag from the top of a nearby box, he pushed Seth aside and carefully wrapped the mouse and trap in it.

"Here." He handed the bundle to the younger prisoner. "Put him in your coat and take him to the cell. Tell Corey that we'll take care of him after work."

"What about the guards?"

"Take off your ID," Jonny instructed. "Tell them you forgot it in your cell and you came back to get it."

Jonny carried the squeegees and mop heads as the three of them left the shop. It felt to him like it had grown colder outside. The sky was darker and he wondered if it would snow again. Seth strode off in the opposite direction, his shoulders hunched upwards and hands buried deep in the pockets of his state-issue coat. Jonny hoped that Daugherty did not see him. If he did, he had no doubt that guards would *kick in* their cell later that night.

"White dudes are crazy," Kevin said, shaking his head as he pushed the wet-vac along the ice-covered street.

"You guys are the crazy ones," Jonny shot back. "That's why so many of you are in prison."

Kevin snorted in Jonny's direction and they fell silent as they continued on their way. They trod carefully over the ice as they turned onto a street that ran alongside the back wall of the prison and led toward a cellhouse that was a twin of the one Jonny lived in. Because of the height of the wall, the street saw little sunlight during the day, even on days when there was sun. More ice accumulated there than elsewhere in the prison.

Jonny watched Kevin as he pushed the wet-vac ahead of him and wondered how he managed sometimes. Not the physical aspect of what he did, but the mental and emotional side of it. He had seventy-five years. Jonny knew that he was in for shooting and killing his best friend, but only because Anton had told him. Kevin never talked about it himself, and Jonny never asked him because he simply assumed that anyone who killed their best friend must have had a damn good reason. Besides, it did not really matter to Jonny what Kevin had done to get sent there—it was the way he carried himself that he respected him for.

Entering Six Wing, Jonny felt the warmth inside the building on his face and hands, and he was grateful for it. He and Kevin ascended a long ramp and halted in front of a steel riot door. A guard looked down on them from the cell-house's main control station. Making them wait long enough to ensure he had impressed on them that he was in control, the guard turned a switch on a control panel and the door slid open.

"Tuck your shirt in, Anderson!"

Jonny tensed and moved past the office quickly, but the voice followed him. "If I see it out again, I'll write you up!"

Her voice reminded Jonny of a crow's. An aggressive caw-like croak, at least whenever she directed it at him. Technically, he knew she was right. It was regulation that prisoners have their shirts tucked in. But guards did not usually make an issue of it while prisoners were working. All guards, that is, except Lessman.

Jonny and Kevin saw Anton as soon as they entered the cell-block. Their crew leader was using a squeegee to lead water away from the bottom of the stairs. He stopped what he was doing and looked at them.

"I was beginning to think you guys weren't going to make it."

Jonny could see he had been busy. His arms glistened with perspiration and it had soaked through his t-shirt in large patches front and back. The ground floor tier gate had a dam of state-issue blankets laid out in front of it to prevent the water from running onto the tiers.

"You should have seen it when I got here," Anton told them, leaning on the handle of the squeegee. "There's no reason they should have let it get this bad."

Jonny noted that his crew leader's t-shirt stuck to him where it had become sodden with sweat, revealing a deeply cut six pack and well-defined chest muscles. This was a source of frustration for Jonny, who had exercised faithfully for as long as he could remember in prison but still was not able to transform his body into anything like that.

"I haven't gotten in there yet," Anton told him, nodding toward the door to the shower room. "I've been trying to clear this area so they can get traffic through."

"We'll get it," Kevin said, leaving the wet-vac and starting the slog toward the shower room through several inches of water.

Jonny followed, noticing for the first time that there were cockroaches in the water. Seeing the ones that were still alive struggle, he did not experience any of the same feelings that had come to him when he saw the trapped mouse. Maybe it was because there were so many of them in that place. He often found them in his bunk, or crawling through his footlocker.

The shower room was a disaster. Soaked towels were strewn everywhere and garbage floated in a lake of floodwater. But no freezing air blasted from the vents like it did in the shower room in the cell-house Jonny lived in. He wondered if the prisoners who lived here realized how good they had it.

Jonny was puzzled by a pair of undershorts floating in the water. He could not fathom a circumstance in which someone would forget them.

"What a bunch of pigs," Kevin remarked, as he surveyed the wreckage.

Jonny waded out to the drain in the center of the floor and used the toe of his boot to push aside the wet mass of garbage covering it. It had no effect. He looked at Kevin.

"My turn?"

Jonny nodded, and Kevin let go a long breath through his teeth.

Jonny made his way through the water toward a bench. Setting the two squeegees he was carrying down, he reached into the bucket and took out a straightened wire hanger that had been formed into a hook at one end. He tossed it to Kevin.

Jonny noted there were two other benches in the room—one more than the cell-house he lived in. As he had a number of times in the past, he wondered how they were split up between blacks and whites. An extra bench did not necessarily mean that prisoners in this cell-house were better off. Odd numbers often caused problems in that place because they were hard to divide.

Jonny watched Kevin feed the end of the hanger into the submerged drain with practiced hands, trying to catch hold of whatever was clogging it. Each movement pushed a surge of water across the room and beneath the door. Jonny thought about how Anton had sealed off the tier gates with blankets.

A wave of water rolled over the step and splashed into the front area when Jonny pushed open the shower room door.

"Hey!'" Anton cast an irritated look in his direction.

"Sorry." Jonny's apology sounded lame, even to him.

Jonny tucked his shirt in on the way to the office. Lessman looked annoyed when he got there. Her ear was pressed to the phone and she turned her head away in an attempt to ignore him. Jonny knew he could not enter the office without her permission, even though the blankets he had come for were stacked on shelves only feet away. He waited at the door.

"No, I didn't get back till three this morning."

Jonny's dislike of her was palpable, to the point that he needed only to call up her image in his mind in order to feel it. But, of course, it was not as simple as that. There was another feeling there, one he understood much less than the first. He felt it rise inside him as he looked at her, leaning as far back in her chair as she could manage, legs cocked up, with the soles of her guard boots pressed against the edge of the desk. His eyes were drawn to the juncture of dark blue polyester stretched over the brazen bulge of her sex, the pliant fabric of her guard pants leaving little to the imagination. Although looking at it only aggravated what he felt. Yet he was unable to pull his eyes away.

He heard her laugh into the phone. A dry cackle. He was fascinated by the way her inseam cut into the hungry mound, dividing it neatly down the center. It brought to his mind the image of an overdeveloped muscle. And perhaps that was it, he thought. Too much exercise. After all, it was no secret that she banged nearly every guard she had ever worked with.

"I got to go," Lessman said, dropping her boots from the edge of the desk and pushing herself upright in the chair. "See you tonight."

She hung up the phone and turned to Jonny. "What?" She spat the word.

Jonny wondered if she sensed what he had been looking at. Or worse, what he had been thinking.

"Can I grab some blankets?"

"No." The guard's response was immediate and looked like it left a rotten taste in her mouth.

Jonny did not doubt that her answer would have been the same no matter what he asked. "We need them for—"

"No! Don't ask again."

Jonny felt his temper rise, and he bit his tongue.

He knew it would cost him his job if he did not. And she would have him taken to the Hole. He could think of a few circumstances when a trip to the Hole could be considered worth it—when the benefit of what was accomplished might outweigh the punishment they would extract for it. But this was not one of them. Not for something that did not really mean anything to him. And not for her either. Jonny turned and left.

Anton saw him before he made it to the shower room. "What's wrong?"

"Nothing." Jonny shook his head as he again pulled his shirt untucked.

"What'd she do?" Anton pressed him, reading Jonny's stress better than he was able to hide it.

"She's an idiot. I just wanted some blankets so I could seal the door like you did with the tier gate."

Anton clapped Jonny on the shoulder and laughed. "You got to know how to talk to her."

"There's only one way to talk to a guard like that."

Anton eyed him critically. "And what do you think that will get you?" Jonny shrugged.

"It's easier than you think," Anton told him. "C'mon, I'll show you."

Jonny hesitated. Under any other circumstance, retracing his steps would not seem like a good idea to him. In fact, it did not seem like a good at that moment. But he trusted Anton. So he followed him.

Lessman's boots were propped against the edge of the desk again, her face hidden behind a newspaper she held up in front of her. Anton entered the office without asking permission. This made Jonny even more uneasy. He again questioned the wisdom of returning there and wondered what kind of abuse she would direct at him when she realized he was back.

"Pearson! Is this what the state pays you for?"

The guard jumped. She flung the paper aside and sprang to her feet, panic on her face. Anton laughed and it startled Jonny to see that Lessman did not seem upset. In fact, she smiled and began to exude an inexplicable warmth. Not directed at him, of course. He did not believe she was even aware that he was there. Standing beside her desk, her attention was solely on Anton. It occurred to Jonny that his crew leader had called her by the name she went by before she married the idiot on third shift.

Anton winked at Jonny. "Why don't you grab some blankets? I think we'll need them."

Jonny did not move. He looked at the guard who did not divert any part of her attention from Anton. There was a strange look in her eyes that seemed to be centered on Anton's midsection where his wet t-shirt clung to the hard muscle of his abdomen. Jonny realized that neither his nor Anton's shirt was tucked in. In his haste to follow his crew leader, he had forgotten to see to it that he was within regulation before he got to the office. Looking again at the guard's eyes, he relaxed. Concern with regulations was not what he saw reflected in them.

Moving past the guard, Jonny began to pull down blankets from the shelves.

"When are you going to do the offices downstairs again?" The guard asked Anton in a thick, whispery voice.

Three bars of pumice stone on a nearby shelf caught Jonny's eye. He palmed one and slipped it into his waistband before leaving the office with an armload of blankets.

On his way back to the shower room, Jonny recalled what Anton had told him about knowing how to talk to her. Bullshit. There had to be more going on there than that. He wondered if his crew leader was boning her. Jonny could not think of anything else that would explain the way she acted. She had literally been squirming as she stood beside the guard desk, mouth agape, as though it were taking everything she had to prevent her overdeveloped muscle from chewing through her pants and coming after what it wanted.

nny was surprised to find Seth in the shower
... Kevin was no longer there, but he had cleared one of the drains before he left and the water level had receded. Seth was pushing the floodwater that remained toward the open drain with a squeegee.

Jonny set the blankets on a bench. They no longer needed them, but he would be damned if he was going to take them back.

"Where'd Kevin go?"

Seth shrugged and continued to herd the water.

Jonny grabbed the other squeegee and set to work across from the young prisoner. Working together, they funneled the water between them toward the open drain. Jonny heard the wet-vac start up somewhere outside the door.

"Any problems getting back to the cell?"

"No." Seth smiled conspiratorily. "I told them I forgot my ID, like you said, and they didn't even search me. I could have been carrying anything."

"What'd Corey say?"

"He was doing a chest piece on Jimm-Dog."

"Shit." Jonny realized that he should have anticipated Corey might be tattooing. It was his day off.

"Was he mad?"

Seth shook his head. "Didn't seem like it. As soon as he saw what I had, he took it."

Jonny set the squeegee aside and grabbed a dustpan from the bucket. A large plastic trash barrel lay on its side near the door. He grabbed that also and began to make his way around the room, scooping trash off the floor with the dustpan and throwing it inside.

"What else we gotta do?" Seth asked, as he pushed the last of the flood water into the drain.

"We've already done more than we had to," Jonny told him. "All they needed was for us to clean it up enough for the plumber to get in here. If he ever does."

Seth bent down and picked up a sopping towel from the floor. Holding it out in front of him, he started toward another.

Jonny frowned. "You're going to end up like Smokey."

Seth dropped the towel and retracted his hand as if it had been burned. He wiped it on his pants, careful to get every finger.

Jonny believed in being cautious. Living the way they had to behind *the Walls*, it was possible to catch a lot of things. In relation to contact with other prisoners' laundry, it was *MRSA* that concerned him most. It was everywhere in the prison. More than a dozen prisoners in every cell-house at any time had the angry red sores that were evidence of the infection. He knew prisoners who had died from it. His friend, Smokey, had almost lost his leg to it. When he got out of the infirmary, it had taken Jonny only one look at his shriveled and scarred leg for him to resolve that he would do all that he could to prevent that from happening to him.

Yet it was not easy, nor always possible, to be as careful as Jonny would have liked. The warden had deemed the issuance of rubber gloves to prisoners a security threat, which made risk at times impossible to avoid. Common sense told him that so many people stacking their clothes and towels together on benches in the prison's shower rooms was not a good idea. But, he had long since accepted that there were simply some things a prisoner could not do anything about.

When Jonny and Seth came out of the shower room, they found the front area cleared of water. Kevin and Anton were seated on the cell-house stairs waiting for them.

Outside, it was lighter than when they had entered the cell-house. The clouds had thinned enough to allow a measure of pale sunlight to filter through. It was not any warmer though. Jonny was glad that the bucket was all that he carried. It enabled him to keep one hand from freezing by alternating it, keeping one in his pocket until the one carrying the bucket became too cold, then switching. His feet slid inside his boots as he walked. Water had soaked into them during the cleanup and he wondered how long it would take for them to freeze solid. He was glad that it was not a long walk back to the shop, because he did not want to find out.

When they neared the gym, Jonny handed the bucket to Seth and split away from the others. He entered through the double doors at the front of the building and spotted the guards just as he came out of the foyer. There were three in the gym office, and they looked up at the same time that he looked at them. Ordinarily, this would not be good. Catching the eye of guards when he was somewhere that he had no business being, doing something that he should not be doing. He was relieved to see them resume their card game. He realized they had only been making sure that he was not Lt. Todd.

Jonny crossed an empty basketball court and came to a stop in front of the equipment room in the back corner of the gym. It was closed off by a gate made from heavy-gauge chain link and secured with a padlock that only the guards in the office could unlock. On the other side of the gate, a Chicano sat on a milk crate, his full attention on the dumbbells in his hands as he alternately lowered and lifted them to the tinny, strangled strains of music emanating from a cheap radio behind him. His choice of music struck Jonny as odd. He had never known a Mexican who liked country before.

"Jonny!" The Chicano greeted him when he noticed that Jonny was there. He set the dumbbells down and got up from the milk crate. Crossing to a cabinet at the back of the room, he returned with a bigger bag of coffee than Jonny had expected.

Jonny estimated there was enough in the bag to last his crew a month. Maybe longer. He reached into his pocket for the stone.

"You wouldn't believe how hard it is to get this," the Chicano said, holding the bag in front of the port cut in the chain link, but not handing it through. "If the *plac-*

as find out someone got them for it, they're going to be mad, *guay*."

Jonny did not say anything. The Chicano was setting him up for something.

"I'm in a bind, Jonny. I got a piece I got to get back to the cell-house before Yard tonight." Jonny maintained his prison face.

"Ain't no way I can get it past *la maquina*, Jonny."

Desperation had crept into the Chicano's voice. It made no difference to Jonny though. If the Chicano wanted to get the knife past a metal detector, it was going to cost him more than a bag of coffee.

The Chicano set the coffee on the window ledge. "If you do this for me, Jonny, I'll give you another one when supplies come in."

Jonny thought about it. "Where do you want it?"

"Eight Wing laundry room. Loco will be there waiting for it."

Jonny looked again at the coffee. He reached out and set the pumice stone beside it. Unzipping his coat, he took the bag and pushed it into his sleeve.

"How's it look?" The Chicano asked.

Jonny surveyed the gym, making sure no one was in sight. He nodded to the Chicano, who handed him a long, narrow package wrapped in paper and sealed with tape. He could tell from the weight and length that it was no slasher. This piece was meant for business. Jonny tucked it into the back of his waistband, double checking to be sure it would not fall out, before pulling the back of his coat over it.

"*Ay- gracias*, Jonny."

Jonny left without saying anything. His mind was busy churning over everything that could go wrong. When he came into view of the office, his heart began to pound and he felt a tightness in his throat. He did not look—he was determined not to make that mistake again. Instead, he did his best to appear as though he were a prisoner who was not hiding a foot-long shank in his pants and a bag of guard coffee in his coat.

Jonny's apprehension eased when he made it out the front door and saw no guards on the frozen street outside. He began to breathe easier.

Back inside the shop, Jonny found Kevin and Seth, but Anton was gone. He tossed the coffee to Kevin, who sat atop an overturned bucket beside the glowing space heater.

"Good lookin' out," Kevin said, weighing the bag in his hand as Jonny swept past.

Jonny retreated into the small bathroom at the back of the shop. The moment the door shut behind him, he shed his coat and hung it on the doorknob. Pulling the shank out, he held it in front of him and studied it. It was bigger than the one they caught him with at the Bay. That one had cost him his *good-time* and two years in *IMU*. Two years he had spent cursing himself for being so stupid, the same way he was cursing himself at that moment. The experience had changed him, but he knew what he was staring at proved that it had not made him any smarter.

He set the knife between his teeth and stepped up onto the stainless steel sink/toilet combination. Reaching up, he pushed against one of the ceiling tiles until it lifted. He slipped the shank into the hollow space above the tile, then let it drop back into place. Stepping down, he looked up and inspected his work.

Taking a half-empty roll of toilet paper from the edge of the sink, he rolled some off into his hand and used it to wipe the rim of the toilet. When he cleaned it to his satisfaction, he unfastened his pants. Turning, he lowered them and sat down.

He preferred to use this bathroom—because it was a bathroom. An actual room with a door he could utilize to shut himself off from the rest of the world inside those walls. As far as he knew, it was the only one still like it in the joint. A hold-over from the old days when those who ran prisons still considered them men—to be deprived of their freedom, certainly, but not to be stripped of all vestiges of dignity, as they were now. There were other bathrooms with doors in the prison, but they were for guards or administrators, and a prisoner caught using one would be taken to the Hole, no matter the excuse.

The bathroom also spared him from having to conduct his business in the cell. He had lived long enough in that place that he had no problem doing it wherever he had to. But this was more than just that, it was time to himself. A few minutes to think—which only someone who has lived for any length of time in overcrowded conditions behind prison walls can understand the unquantifiable value of. Other prisoners did not have this time. Unless, of course, they were sent to IMU, in which case, time to oneself was no longer an indulgence. It was punishment wielded against them.

He had been in prison less than six months when they asked him to pack a piece out to the Yard. He was a duck and they took advantage of that. They told him that he was the last person the guards would search and, if he did it, everyone would know what a stand-up guy he was.

As it turned out, the guards did search him, and they sent him to IMU. The prison administrator who conducted his hearing knew the shank was not his. He gave Jonny the opportunity to tell who gave it to him, but he refused. In the neighborhood he came from, telling was not considered honorable. And he had been in prison long enough to know that it was not a safe place for someone who did not know how to keep his mouth shut.

They started his "program" then. That was the word the prison administrator used to describe what they did to him. The reality of it was that they buried him, in a concrete coffin in a cemetery full of others who, like him, felt no different than if they were dead. Perhaps they were and just did not know it. It was impossible to sort out what was real and what was not in that place.

Every day was a hundred years, every week a thousand.

Who knew what a day was in there anyway? There was no clock to divide it into increments. And daytime was indistinguishable from night. The din never ebbed, nor the sterile, all-invasive artificial light.

And yet, he knew that time did pass because he observed its effect on those locked in cells around him. It affected each of them differently in accordance with their individual capacity to endure what was being done to them. It destroyed some. Peeling away layers of their sanity one at a time until nothing remained but the frightened, irrational beast at their core, leaving them to spend their days ramming their heads against the steel door of their cell, laughing and shouting hysterically or painting themselves and the walls with shit. Jonny had even seen some of these prisoners make it to their release date—the end date of the time they were sentenced to serve in prison. Guards came and took them away. But he found it hard to believe that they actually released them. How could they? How do you do that to someone? Take them over the edge of sanity, then release them into the freeworld. What sense does it make to do that?

Others he had seen there chose to destroy themselves, exchanging their concrete box for a state-issue body bag in a carefully deliberated act. Preferring it to allowing the madness to overtake them.

A seventeen-year-old prisoner named Clark lived for six months in the cell next to Jonny. Until the day Jonny saw guards haul him out and dump him on the floor in front of his cell. The image of the sheet cinched around his neck and the swollen face locked in a grimace was burned indelibly into Jonny's mind.

Jonny had felt the same demonic shadow that devoured Clark weighing down on his own shoulders. He realized that he had to find a way to make it in there, or there was no doubt he would succumb to it too. The problem was that there was no instruction book, nothing to teach a prisoner how to survive it. A prisoner either found a way, or he did not. It was all the same to the people who put him in there.

Jonny withdrew into himself and searched for a way to survive. He found it in unmitigated acceptance of the small cell he was locked inside of as the extent of his universe. Embracing it, he trained himself to want nothing more. For him there was nothing more.

A small community of ants living in a crack in the concrete floor became his friends, his companions, his comrades. Caretakers of his sanity. Whenever he moved in the cell, he was careful not to harm them. He fed and cared for them. In the absence of anything else, they became his reason for existence. His own individual life no longer really a concern. Until, the day when the steel door at the front of his universe slid open and guards told him that he could go.

He remembered his first thought. That he could not leave. Not then. Who would look out for the ants?

Leaving was harder than getting put in. Two years had passed and he had turned twenty, but he felt like an old man. Outside the confined space that he had accepted as his entire world, he felt vulnerable, naked, exposed. A turtle without a shell.

Daylight hurt his eyes and kept him in a constant squint. Looking anywhere other than down made him reel. Nauseous. He felt like a speck in relation to the infinite space around him.

He did not have much fat reserve to begin with, but the years of meager rations stole that from him and more. His bones were his most prominent feature.

His legs quavered beneath him. It was many months before he was able to stop trembling. He looked anemic, his skin pale to the point of translucence.

And speaking was difficult. For a long time, he did not want to speak to anyone. Even now, he spoke less than he had before they put him in that place.

The experience had changed him irreversibly. Not

in a half-hearted or transitory way either. It had shaken him to the very center of his being.

Even now, he did not step on ants.

Jonny also knew that prison officials had lobbied for and gotten a new law enacted since the time he had been in IMU. The state could now add ten years to a prisoner's sentence if he was caught with a weapon. But the threat of more time did not mean much to him. He had been locked up since he was seventeen, and he was now twenty-seven. What difference would ten more years make?

He did not know what it would be like to get out of prison. Sometimes he thought about it. More often as his release date got closer. But he did not know firsthand. Behind the Walls, the freeworld did not seem real, and the longer he spent behind them, the further away and more unreal it seemed. Where he was at that moment, that was real. He had a sense that when he did get released, he would feel like he did when they let him out of IMU. He would leave if they let him out, of course. But if they did not, he could deal with it. If there was one thing he knew about—knew firsthand with no doubt about his ability to deal with it, or ignorance of what he could expect—it was how to live in that place. He had been doing it a long time. And for however long it was necessary, he knew he would continue to do it.

He did harbor a fear. But it was not related to more time in prison. What he feared was being buried alive. He had promised himself that he would never allow them to put him in that place again. And, again recalling the image of Clark's tortured, dead face, he knew exactly how he would prevent them from doing it if he had to.

He realized that he did not need to use the bathroom. Standing up, he refastened his pants. He no longer felt like being alone.

Back out in the shop, Jonny sat down next to the heater and surrendered to its warmth, while Kevin and

Seth readied the equipment they would need that afternoon. Bending forward, he untied his boots and kicked them off. Stripping off his socks, he wrung them out and draped them over the heater. As he pushed his boots closer to the heat, the front door banged open and Anton entered, letting in a gust of icy air that Jonny felt instantly on his unclad feet.

"It's starting to warm up out there," Anton said, closing the door with a backward push of his foot.

Jonny eyed his crew leader's coat as he crossed the shop. It was nice, not state-issue like the one Jonny and most other prisoners behind those walls wore. Anton never wore state-issue. He did not have to. Despite the fact that he had been in prison for more than twenty years, he had a girl who sent him clothing packages and visited him each week. Jonny had even seen her once, when a bathroom flooded in the Visiting Room and he was called out to clean it up. She was beautiful.

Jonny watched steam curl upward from his socks. As he turned them over, he tried to imagine what it would be like if he had a girl who came to visit him.

"Coffee's hot," Kevin announced, breaking up the scene in Jonny's mind.

"Where'd we get it?" Anton asked.

Kevin nodded in Jonny's direction as he filled his cup.

Seth carried over a pair of cups and handed one to Jonny before sitting down on a milk crate beside him.

"Jonny comes through again," Anton said, cradling a cup in his hands.

"We ain't going to have it this good when he gets out," Kevin said.

Their words made Jonny feel good. A comfortable silence settled over all of them briefly, until Anton shattered it.

"You know what you're going to do when you get out?"

Jonny was instantly uncomfortable. He knew he

was the only one of them that would ever get out, and he did not like to think about it when he was with them. It seemed somehow disrespectful. He stared hard at the steam rising from his socks. Why did Anton have to ask him that? It was not important—at least, in relation to what was between them. What they were doing at that moment, that was what mattered. Not losing touch with that was how he had learned to do his time, to make it as long in there as he had. This was the only reality he had known since he was a teenager.

Jonny shrugged, not saying anything.

"I'd sign on with a crab boat. Where I'm from..."

"You ain't going to sign on with shit," Kevin said, cutting Seth off. "Nothin' outside these walls anyway. You ain't gonna get out."

"Things could change."

"No, they can't," Kevin said, his face hardening. "Things don't happen in here for nobody. The sooner a motherfucker faces up to it, the better. If you ain't got money, your ass is stayin' in here for the duration with the rest of us."

Jonny noticed that Seth was no longer looking at any of them, he stared at the floor. He did not have to pretend to know how the younger prisoner felt—he knew very well. A twelve-year sentence is the same as forever to a seventeen year old. It was not until Jonny had made it more than halfway through his sentence that it began to dawn on him that he might be able to make it the rest of the way. The difference between him and Seth was that the younger prisoner was never going to reach a point in his sentence when that realization would come to him. Kevin was right. But Jonny still thought he was an asshole for saying it.

The door to the office opened and Mr. Marks appeared in the doorway, a phone held to his ear as he waved them off. That was the signal. Time for them to return to their cells for count.

Jonny took his socks off the heater. They were not

dry, but he relished their warmth as he pulled them on. Seth waited for him while he slipped on his boots and tied them. They were warm too.

Jonny and Seth left the shop together, merging into the line of prisoners on the street. Not all work crews had to return for count. Some, like Matt's, were counted where they worked. But Jonny's, like many others, made the trek back to the cell-houses every day at this time.

As Jonny passed beneath the roll-up gate at the center of the prison, he decided that Anton was wrong about it starting to warm up. It had not by any noticeable degree anyway. The cold made him thankful for the warmth inside his boots.

Ahead, Jonny saw the entrance to Eight Wing. He had often thought that the old building looked like a monster, its entrance a gaping mouth greedily devouring the stream of prisoners entering it. He wondered how many it had taken into its belly since it was built. Surveying the weathered brick and crumbling mortar of its face, he wondered how many more it would in the future. Would it still be there in another 100 years? Would it still swallow men and still shit them out?

An electronic screech pierced the frozen expanse of the courtyard, the not unfamiliar sound bringing everyone to a halt.

"Against the wall! Get against the wall now!" The angry bark of the guard in the tower was amplified and spit at them through a bullhorn.

Everyone in the courtyard knew the drill. They moved off the course and lined up with their backs against the outer wall of the building that housed the Chowhall, although doing it slower than if they had been asked in a civil tone. Jonny did not understand why guards felt it necessary to talk like that. Did they actually believe it made prisoners more receptive to doing what they were told?

Everyone waited, their eyes trained on the entrance

of the cell-house. The tower guard held his position on the catwalk outside his tower, rifle ready. A minute later, the door burst outward and three guards exited, pulling a skinhead between them. Cuffed behind his back and wearing only a t-shirt, boxer shorts, and shower shoes, he looked upset. Too upset to register the cold. The group covered a dozen yards before the door flew open again and more guards appeared with another skinhead. Everyone in the courtyard remained silent as the two prisoners were marched forward. Even the trio of young skinheads not far from Jonny and Seth held their tongues.

As the guards made their way across the ice-covered court-yard, Jonny saw the guard in the lead turn his attention toward a pair of black prisoners who were not as close to the side of the building as he thought they should be.

"Get against the wall! Move!" He used the same tone and demeanor the tower guard had moments earlier.

The tower guard turned his rifle toward the two prisoners, who quickly pressed their backs against the building.

The guards rounded the corner at the end of the Chowhall and disappeared. But, still, no one moved. Not until the announcement came through the bullhorn a minute later.

"Resume movement."

Inside the cell-house, Jonny and Seth joined the end of a long line of prisoners waiting to pass through the metal detector. At first Jonny thought that someone might have been *stuck*, but looking through the crowd he realized the jam had formed because Nieukoot and two other guards were pat-searching every prisoner after they passed through the detector.

"Jesus Christ. That's all they do in this place is search us."

Jonny was glad to hear Seth speak. He had not said

anything since Kevin had said what he had. Jonny wondered if this meant the young prisoner was over it.

When it was their turn to pass through the detector, Jonny and Seth stepped through and stood for search, spreading their feet and holding their arms out from their sides. Jonny was glad that he did not have to go to Nieukoot. The poor bastard behind him did. On the way up the stairs, Jonny saw that Nieukoot was still searching him, feeling the length of every seam as though he believed there was a possibility he might find something.

The door of their cell opened before they reached it.

"I was beginning to think they'd hauled you guys off," Corey said, pivoting his giant frame on the tiny bunk and sitting up as they entered.

Jonny sat down on Matt's bunk to untie his boots. "They searched everyone on the way in. It took forever."

"Where's the mouse?" Seth asked, looking around the cell.

Corey nodded toward the laundry bucket in the back of the cell and the young prisoner went to it.

"Sorry about sending him back," Jonny said. "I didn't think about you working in here."

Corey waved it off. "I had to cut it short anyway. The toads downstairs screamed at each other all morning. The Man kept walking the tier."

"O-w-w-w!"

Seth leapt up from where he crouched over the laundry bucket. He held one of his fingers, trying to pinch off the flow of fresh blood.

"The little fucker bit me."

Jonny laughed and joined Seth in the back of the cell. Looking in the bucket, he was surprised to see that the mouse was free of the trap.

"How'd you get him out?"

"It wasn't easy," Corey said. "And he's still got a lot of that stuff on him. I was hoping he could lick it off, or whatever it is they do to clean themselves."

Jonny lowered himself onto a knee and looked closer. Resin still clung to the mouse in many places and, when Jonny poked at him with a finger, he could see that his feet were gummed up as well. The little animal could hardly move and looked exhausted.

"He won't get that off by himself."

"We'll have to figure out a way to do it then," Corey said, rising from his bunk. Squeezing in beside Jonny, he reached into the bucket and picked up the mouse.

"He bites," Seth warned, extracting the wounded finger from his mouth in order to speak.

"What makes you so sure it's a 'he'?" Corey asked, holding the mouse close to his chest. "You looked at his junk?"

"N-o-o."

"You did something," Corey said. "I worked on him for an hour to get him out of that trap and he didn't bite me."

"All I did was reach into the bucket," Seth insisted. "I didn't even touch him and he bit me."

Enclosed in Corey's giant hand with only its head protruding, the mouse looked relaxed to Jonny. Certainly not like a creature prone to sudden fits of aggression.

Taking a bottle cap from the table, Jonny filled it with water from the sink and placed it in the bucket. Seeing what he had done, Corey set the mouse down next to the makeshift bowl. It responded immediately. Holding onto the cap with its tiny gummed up forepaws, it licked thirstily at the water.

"Look at him," Seth said. "He's thirstier than hell."

The three of them huddled around the bucket and watched the mouse drink. When it was finished, it dipped its forepaws in the water and began to try to clean them.

"He's kind of cool," Seth said.

"I'd still like to know how you know it's a 'he'."

"I just guessed."

"Yeah, right."

The cell-house loudspeakers crackled to life. "Count-time! Count!"

They left the mouse and went to their bunks. Corey laid down and opened a book he had been working on for more than a month. Turning to face the wall, he began to read.

Above him, Seth lay on his bunk and stared at the ceiling, as had become his habit at count-time. Jonny knew what he was doing, and also that he would cease to do it eventually. His thoughts of the freeworld would become exhausted as his mind comprehended over time that they were really only illusions, mental constructions that no longer had a connection to his physical reality, nor ever would again. First, they would become painful to contemplate and he would begin to eschew them. Eventually, he would cease to generate them altogether. Jonny knew that it was not a matter of if this would happen, but when.

Stretching out on his bunk, Jonny reached beneath the mattress pad and pulled out a car magazine. Opening to the dog-eared layout of a Mustang, he studied the car from one end to the other. He loved to look at it, despite the incongruity it posed to his life. Before he was sent to prison, he had never owned a car, nor had a driver's license. It seemed strange to him that this car, this object that had no practical application to his life, held the power to draw him to it.

Guards appeared in front of their cell, Nieukoot and two others. Jonny pretended not to see them, the same as Corey and Seth were doing. The guards marked their countboards and moved on, the two shadows staying close on Nieukoot's heels.

Jonny returned his attention to the magazine, but he was no longer able to concentrate on it. The question Anton asked him earlier weighed on his mind. What was he going to do when he got out? Would he be able to get a job? What kind of job could he get if he did not know how to do anything?

"That guy's a fucking asshole."

The words brought Jonny back. He was not sure what Seth was talking about. "They're all assholes," Corey said. "If you don't expect anything more from them than that, then you won't be disappointed."

"He's trying to start a problem," Seth persisted.

"Maybe you shouldn't have come to prison," Corey offered. Jonny listened, but stayed out of the exchange.

"I didn't have a choice," Seth grumbled.

Sensing resentment in the young prisoner's voice, Corey set his book aside and got up from his bunk. "Didn't have a choice? You didn't have a choice? You blew somebody's head off."

"I didn't shoot anyone."

"You were there. You're as guilty as Brady."

"It doesn't matter," Jonny said, feeling compelled to intervene at this point. "We all got to deal with what we got to deal with. None of us can change it by looking back."

"I just don't understand it," Corey said, turning to Jonny. "Everytime they've sent me to prison, it was for trying to 'come up.' For trying to better my situation, you know what I mean? The first time was for robbery. Now, cooking dope. I can understand that kind of crime. Not randomly shooting someone for no reason. That don't make no sense to me."

Jonny noticed that Seth had returned to staring at the ceiling.

"I don't see what he did as being much different than what I'm in here for," Jonny said. Corey shook his head. "That was different."

"I don't think it was. The truth is, sometimes young people do stupid things. They don't think before they act."

Corey again shook his head, but he did not say anything.

"Not everyone's got the kind of street hustle you

got, Corey."

A smile lit the oversized prisoner's face. Jonny had touched on a subject close to his heart.

"It ain't that hard, Jonny. I learned it the first time I was in the joint and, when I got out, I was making more money than I could spend. That's a good feeling, Jonny—the best fuckin' feeling in the world."

The clamor of cell doors opening on the tier below them reverberated through the block. Jonny slipped the car magazine beneath his mattress pad and jumped down from his bunk. Sitting on the lower bunk, he put on his boots.

"What order are they running the tiers?" Corey asked as he splashed water on his face at the sink.

The door of their cell began to open.

"Never mind," he said, reaching for his towel.

Jonny was out on the tier the moment the door opened wide enough for him to get through and he did not turn to look for Seth until he was halfway across the courtyard. When he saw that the young prisoner was not among the line of prisoners behind him, he continued on his way.

They usually ate together, although Jonny did not wait for him that day because he thought it was best to give him some breathing room. Some time to work out what was going on inside of him. He did not mind looking out for Seth, but there was a limit to what he could do. He could show him how to live there, how to make it inside the Walls, but he could not give him the strength he would need in order to do it. Every one of the fifty-three years he was sentenced to were his own and no one else could do them for him.

Inside the Chowhall, Jonny recognized the hulking figure of Sgt. O'Riley on the shooting balcony overhead. Looking down on prisoners as they lined up for trays, he scrutinized them a face at a time. He was the prison gang specialist. On his say-so alone, prisoners were sent to IMU for terms of indefinite confinement. Jonny felt the tension his presence created. Conversations were more subdued, expressions more grave. No one wanted to be noticed, and that included Jonny. He pushed the stocking cap lower on his brow as he joined the line, and he was careful not to look up. He was not a gang member, but he knew that made no difference. A prisoner was part of whatever Sgt. O'Riley said he was. And once he said it, there was no way you could say otherwise.

As he neared the counter, Jonny saw they were having turkey. It was the second time that week. The agent who purchased food for the prison labeled it turkey, but it was really a jelled paste of ground sludge that may or may not have ever been part of a turkey. If it had, it was from parts not meant to be eaten. Living so long in prison, Jonny found that he could stomach nearly anything. Not this though. The first time the prison had given it to them, it had knocked nearly 100 prisoners off the line, keeping them in their bunks sick as dogs for a week.

Jonny took the tray pushed out to him through the narrow slot beneath the window and moved down the counter. Behind the next window, a heavyset Native American ladled soup into small plastic bowls. He pushed half-bowls of watery soup through the slot. Setting one on his tray, Jonny waited for him to push another out.

On the other side of the glass, the prisoner did not move, his pockmarked face a mask. Jonny knew his name was Chief, although he thought Police Chief would have suited him better. He wanted to say something, but a guard stood sentry over the line a short distance away.

Jonny shrugged as though it did not matter one way or the other to him and moved down the counter. When the Native slid a bowl through the slot for the next guy in line, Jonny turned back quickly. Excusing himself to the prisoner in front of the window, he took the bowl and set it on his tray. Now the Native looked as though he wanted to say something, but Jonny did not care. He had what he wanted.

Claude looked up as Jonny sat down across from him. "What's up?"

Jonny shrugged. "Nothing."

Jonny saw that his friend had already eaten everything on his tray, except the turkey. Lifting one of his bowls of soup to his lips, he drank, surprised it was still warm.

Seth arrived and dropped heavily onto a stool. He ate without saying anything. None of them said anything.

As Jonny finished the first bowl, he reflected on the three of them seated at the table.

His friend Claude. Hanging out as long as he could in the Chowhall in order to delay the inevitable, the point in time when he would have to return to work and again freeze his ass off.

Seth. Trying to find his bearings in a life that had been fucked off before it had even really begun.

And himself. Jonny wondered what could be considered his source of misery. Lifting the second bowl of soup to his lips, no thought of what it might be came to him. Drinking the tepid liquid in a handful of swallows, he realized there was nothing but broth in this bowl either.

A tray clattered to the floor somewhere to his left, and Jonny turned toward it. Everyone did. Even the guards' guns swung in that direction. But it was nothing more than what it sounded like. Someone had dropped their tray on the way to the dishtank. The tension ebbed and the din of a thousand conversations began anew.

Returning his attention to the table, Jonny took a paper napkin from the short stack in front of him and was startled to see several silverfish spill out.

"Goddamn it." Claude snickered.

Jonny shook out the remaining napkins and found more of the bugs inside. Sweeping them off the table, he sent them scurrying for a new home.

"You ready to get out of here?"

Claude shook his head. "Nah, I'll probably stick around awhile longer."

Jonny did not blame him. He would stay there until they kicked him out, too, if he had Claude's job. Nodding to his friend, he rose from the table and departed. Seth picked up his tray and followed.

Near the door, Jonny slid his tray through a slot in the wall leading into the dish tank and turned toward the exit.

"Stand for search."

He froze, knowing what was expected of him. The command had been issued by one of the half dozen guards deployed in front of the door leading outside. Stealing a glance at him, Jonny was relieved to see that he was not one he had ever had a problem with. Turning his back, Jonny pulled the cap from his head and raised his arms. As the guard's hands made their way over him, Jonny heard another "stand for search"command, this one issued in a gruffer, more aggressive tone. Out of the corner of his eye, he saw that Seth had not been able to make it out the door unmolested either.

Jonny realized that it was his fault he was pulled over. If he would have been paying attention, he would have timed it better. Walking out without being part of a crowd of others trying to do the same thing at the same time was asking for a search.

"Unzip the coat."

It was the thickset guard behind Seth. This second command no less aggressive than his first.

Seth lowered his arms to unzip his coat, then raised them again. Lifting the back of the coat, the guard peered beneath.

"Hands behind your back."

"What?" Seth was dumbfounded.

"Do not turn around," the guard said, the threat implicit in his voice. The dull glint of a pair of handcuffs appeared in one of his hands and he grabbed Seth's wrist from behind with the other. All of the guards moved to position themselves around him. Even the guard searching Jonny ceased what he was doing and joined them.

"I've warned you before for not having your shirt tucked in," the guard said, ratcheting the cuffs onto the young prisoner's wrists.

Seth shook his head. Not in denial but disgust. He had no control over what was happening to him, and he knew it. Nothing he could say or do would change anything, except possibly for the worse.

Gripping the cuffs at the point at which they were linked together, the guard pushed him forward. "Move."

As a trio of guards led Seth out of the Chowhall, Jonny started toward the door. "Wait."

The command came from behind, and he halted without looking back. A moment later, he heard the voice again.

"All right, go ahead."

Outside, Jonny saw that the blanket of clouds overhead had grown darker and a gust had risen. Inside the prison's walls the wind swirled making it impossible to tell which direction it came from. Jonny pulled the zipper of his coat up as far as it would go and tucked his chin into the collar. Pushing his hands into the refuge of his pockets, he wondered if it would snow again. It looked like it.

On his way back to the shop, Jonny replayed in his mind what the guard said about having previously told Seth to tuck in his shirt. Jonny could not remember him ever doing that. At least Seth had not tried to argue, he thought. It was possible they would only take him to the holding cell across from the Shift Office. If that was the case, they would leave him there until after the Chowhall cleared, then return and give him the third degree. If they were still unable to provoke a confrontation, they might let him go. Jonny knew this because of the times it had happened to him. It was not pleasant but still better than the Hole.

Jonny found the front door of the shop unlocked. Peering inside, he saw that Mr. Marks was in his office, but Kevin and Anton had not yet returned. He pushed the door closed again and sat down on the cart outside, the same place he and Seth had waited earlier that morning. Taking the tobacco pouch from his pocket, he removed a pinch and pressed it into a rolling paper. Hunching forward over the paper to protect it from the wind, he began to roll it into a cigarette.

"You got one of those I could get?"

Jonny looked up. He had been concentrating on what he was doing, unaware anyone was approaching. Fingerless Tony stood in front of him, and Jonny wondered if he had seen the pouch. Licking the end of the paper and pressing it down, he eyed the weasel-faced prisoner. Pinching a stray strand of tobacco from the end of the newly made cigarette, he realized that it did not really matter to him if Tony had seen the pouch or not. It would not change what he was going to tell him.

"This one's all I got."

Tony's face tightened into a scowl as Jonny's eyes bore into his. The older prisoner turned and headed off in the direction of the gym.

He had nerve, Jonny thought, as he watched him go. Settling the cigarette between his lips, he felt in his pocket with cold-bitten fingers for his matchbook. Lighting up behind cupped hands, he puffed a cloud of blue-tinged smoke that was whisked away by the wind.

Jonny was not stingy. It simply struck him as wrong that Tony would try to bum anything from him. Jonny knew that he could get a job if he wanted one. Not his old job at the metal plant, of course, but there were other things he could do if he had not become so settled into making a living off getting others to feel sorry for him. And if he did work, he would be allowed to keep what he earned, which was more than Jonny had going for himself. Like most prisoners there, Jonny never saw the thirty dollars he earned each month for working full time. It was seized and put toward his state-imposed debt (or, as the state called it, his "Legal Financial Obligation"). He was not even sure how much it was anymore, nor did he see the sense in trying to keep track because it was more than he could hope to ever pay. All he knew for certain was that the amount compounded at a 12 percent, twice-a-year rate, much faster than could be paid down with the paltry sum they took from him. The only real income Jonny had was what he was able to earn smuggling contraband from one part of the joint to another, or what Corey kicked him for assisting in his hustles. Living like he had to there, it was hard for him to feel sorry for Tony, even if the state did steal his fingers.

The state had imposed the debt on Jonny for a number of reasons, namely: restitution and fines, a hospital bill, and the fee for his public defender. The latter was the charge he considered the most unfair.

Jonny's public defender was a truck. Juggling dozens of cases at once, Jonny doubted that he would have had the ability to prepare a reasonable defense even if he had only one. The only time Jonny saw him for more than five minutes was the day before his trial, and even then the public defender did not listen to him. During the trial, he simply sat there intermittently touching the tip of a pen to a blank legal pad in front of him. But he never even wrote anything down. On the other side of the courtroom, the prosecution's table was manned by three deputy prosecutors and, in the rows behind them, an army of policemen and detectives. Occasionally the public defender reacted to testimony by raising his eyebrows, but he did not object. Jonny felt that it was not right to stick him with an attorney bill when they did not give him a real attorney.

The hospital bill, on the other hand, he supposed was legitimate. He could not dispute it, although it did not sit right with him either when he thought about it.

The cops shot him and he had nearly died. Why should he have to pay for that?

And at sentencing, the judge added court fees and restitution to the debt. A final kick in the stomach before sending him to prison. To Jonny, it seemed no different than continuing to beat someone who was already dead. What was the point? He knew from Anton that things had not always been the way they were, that the amount of time a person was sentenced to serve in prison used to be enough. Jonny wished it was still that way. He could not think of a circumstance where he might ever be able to pay what he owed. And a part of him was fine with that—the part that felt the state could fuck itself. But the debt worried him in relation to being released from prison. He would have preferred to think that getting out would mean a new start, completion of his sentence. But he knew there would never be an end to what he had been sentenced to.

An image of Eric Clayton pushed into Jonny's mind. He's the motherfucker who should have to pay, Jonny thought. The last time Jonny saw him had been at the trial, and he wondered what Eric's life was like now. He imagined that he was married and lived in a nice house. No doubt had a good job at the aircraft manufacturing company his father worked for. He probably did not even think about Jonny anymore.

Jonny had fantasized a thousand times about getting out and tracking Eric down. He thought about what it would be like to be able to make him pay, take everything he had, or in some other way force him to atone for what he had done. Or maybe do what he now wished he would have done when he had the chance—blow Eric Clayton's rotten head clean off his shoulders. It was a sentiment Jonny harbored for no one else in the world, but Eric held a special place in his heart.

To be fair, it had not all been just Eric. It was his friends, too, although Jonny held Eric responsible because he was the reason they did what they did. He had become fixated on Jonny, finding great satisfaction in persecuting him in front of everyone at the high school they went to together. Jonny often wondered what it was that had made Eric pick him out of the more than 2,000 other kids at the school. Many times he had wished someone else would catch Eric's attention and, in doing so, inherit at least some of the abuse he reserved for Jonny. It never happened though.

Eric had used to call him "Dirt Boy." Jonny did not know why he had come up with that name. It was not that he was dirty. He wasn't. But it had made him feel like dirt, no doubt about that.

He had fought Eric twice. Not because he believed that he could beat him. Eric was nearly a foot taller, seventy-five pounds heavier, and played defensive end on the varsity football team. Jonny had merely hoped that by fighting he might win enough respect that Eric would leave him alone.

The first fight was over almost before it had started. Jonny caught one in the eye with enough force behind it to lift him off his feet and sit him down hard. By the time he was able to pull himself up off the ground, Eric and his friends were gone. Jonny had not even gotten off a punch.

He had stayed away from school for two weeks because his eye was swollen shut. When the swelling had gone down enough for him to return, he discovered that his attempt to fight had not won him anything. On the contrary, the abuse got worse.

He and Eric had went at it again a week later, when Eric pushed him on the stairs at the back of the school. Apparently he had concluded that physically assaulting Jonny was as much fun, if perhaps not more, than the other kinds of abuse he heaped on him. Reacting on impulse, Jonny had launched himself at his tormentor and fought with everything he had, including his teeth. The second fight had lasted longer, although its outcome was no different than the first. Jonny was overpowered and pinned to the ground. Eric bashed him in the face hard several times, then spit on him in front of everyone watching. It was then, in that moment of utter defeat and hopelessness, that Jonny had realized what he would do. What he had to do.

He had brought the gun to school the next day, a snub-nosed .357 his mother kept beneath her mattress. She did not know that he knew where it was, but he had since he was thirteen, when he had found it while snooping around her room one evening after she left for work.

A smile creased Jonny's frozen face as he remembered what Eric had done when he pulled out the gun in the cafeteria and pointed it at him. The words Jonny had spoken to him at the time were calm and even.

"You're dead, Eric."

The bully ran like a bitch. Like the frightened little bitch that Jonny always knew he was. It was an image Jonny held onto, his greatest victory. He also remembered what he felt at the time because it, too, was an inherent part of the memory. Exuberance. Exhilaration. And, at last, no fear. In that moment, he feared no one. He had laughed in relief, and kept laughing. No wonder so many witnesses at his trial had described him as a madman.

Jonny had pointed the gun at the others too, Eric's friends. Seated at their lunch table, they had been trapped. Too scared to run. He screamed at them, "Who's Dirt Boy now?!"

Jonny had still been laughing when the bullet tore into his belly. He didn't even see it coming. The Seattle police officer assigned to the school had fired from thirty feet away. He remembered laying bleeding and unmoving on the floor. The screaming and chaos around him like a movie. Not real. Certainly not one he was playing a part in.

Getting shot was worse than getting the wind knocked out of him. Much worse. Worse even than getting his face beat in by Eric Clayton. It was not like on TV. "Stop or I'll shoot!" "Freeze!" "Hands up!" "Drop the weapon!" None of that. Curled on the floor, his stomach on fire and blood pulsing out of his wound and through his hands, Jonny had realized the truth. In real life, cops don't tell you anything. They just shoot.

Jonny flipped away the stub of his cigarette and shook his hand in pain. He had let it burn down too far. He noticed several small snowflakes drift down around him. Getting to his feet, he went inside.

Jonny was pushing a large floor-scrubbing machine out from the back of the shop when Anton and Kevin walked in. Kevin set to work loading a cart with what they would need for their next job.

"Where's the kid?"

Uncapping one of the floor machine's twin ten-gallon tanks, Jonny shrugged. "They hauled him out of the Chowhall."

"They take him to the Hole?"

Jonny poured a slug of cleaning solution into the tank and shrugged again. "I don't know," he said, settling the tank's lid back into place. "It didn't look good."

A furrow appeared on Anton's brow, but he said nothing. He and Jonny both knew there was not anything they could do for the young prisoner.

The three of them left the shop together. Anton leading, carrying mops over his shoulder. Kevin pushing the cart behind him. And Jonny following with the floor machine, struggling to keep up as the soles of his boots slipped on the ice. The disadvantage of his lack of seniority in this circumstance did not escape him. He knew that if Seth were there, their loads would be apportioned differently. Anton would likely not be carrying anything, Kevin would get the mop handles, Jonny would push the cart, and Seth would be stuck with the floor machine. They did not, of course, plot it out like that. It was simply the natural order. Jonny wondered if it was the same on job sites in the freeworld.

Anton and Kevin were no longer in sight by the time Jonny neared the roll-up gate at the center of the prison. He had to fight harder for traction there because the walkway sloped upwards. The floor machine rolled well on flat floors, but trying to push it outdoors was a bitch. More so when it was as cold and icy as it was. As Jonny strained to keep the machine moving forward, a door to the left of the security gate opened and he looked up.

Seth walked toward him smiling.

"I thought you were booked," Jonny said, giving up the effort to push the machine, although he braced himself against it so that it would not roll back down the slope.

"They brought in a couple kitchen workers for *pruno*," Seth said, getting in beside Jonny, prepared to help him push. "They had to kick me loose."

"Oh, no," Jonny chuckled, shaking his head as he stepped back from the machine, letting Seth take it.

"I've already pushed more than my share. Your turn."

They caught up to Anton outside One Wing.

"Where'd you find him?" the crew leader asked Jonny.

"Apparently the guards don't want him, so we're stuck with him."

Anton held the door as Seth wrestled the floor machine, banging it loudly against the steel-and-brick door frame. Putting his shoulder into it, the young prisoner pushed while Jonny guided the machine from the front. Once they were inside, Anton let the heavy door slam shut and waved a hand at the dark glass of the control booth. The barred gate in front of them slid open, and they moved further into the building.

The cell-house they were in was designed differently than any other in the prison. Built in the 1950s, it was the newest and, despite a height of only two stories, it sprawled over a lot of ground. Prison officials used the north side of the building as the Hole, and the side Jonny's crew had entered for elderly, infirm, and disabled convicts.

They stopped in front of a long tier of cells at the end of the cell-house's central corridor. Jonny could see that Kevin had already been there. The equipment and supplies he had pushed over on the cart were lined up on the floor in front of the tier gate.

"Corky!" Anton hailed a short, gray-haired guard who had stepped into view at the opposite end of the corridor.

The guard smiled when he saw them. "Don't be yelling in my cell-house," he chided them good-naturedly as he approached. "You'll wake up the old folks, and we'll have a riot on our hands."

Anton laughed. "Corky, you're the only one who sleeps in here at this time of day."

"Anderson... Morgan..." The guard nodded to Jonny and Seth as he passed them, unclipping an overloaded ring of keys from his belt.

Jonny liked this guard, whose real name was O'Leary. He felt that if there was such a thing as a decent guard, he was it. O'Leary came to work to put in his eight hours, nothing more.

The guard unlocked and slid open the tier gate. The sound of the heavy gate moving on its massive steel runner reverberated down the tier.

"Thanks Corky," Anton told him. "Can you open the ones upstairs too? Kevin's already up there."

"Should I let the porter out?" Anton looked at Jonny.

"Uh, that's okay," Jonny said. "We got it."

The guard shrugged and left.

The sound of running water came from a utility room off the corridor. Seth was filling the mop buckets they would need.

"You can take the machine," Jonny said. "We can get it clean enough with a mop. The old people in here don't make enough traffic to get the floor dirty."

Anton looked at him a moment before nodding assent. As he pushed the floor machine toward the freight elevator at the end of the corridor, Jonny went to find a broom.

As he swept the tier, Jonny was reminded of what he disliked most about this cell-house. There was no ventilation. None that worked anyway. The still air reeked of infirmity and senescence. Like most of the prisoners sealed away in that building, it never went anywhere.

It was also quiet, which Jonny did not like either. He did not mind when the clamor inside his own cell-house subsided enough late at night that he could begin to hear himself think. But this was like a morgue. It was also why he did not like to use the floor machine there. The machine was noisy, and running it for any length of time in that place made him feel the same as he suspected one might if they were pushing a roaring lawnmower through a graveyard. As he made a final pass down the tier stirring up dust with the broom, he broke the silence with a sneeze.

Seth met him at the head of the tier with the mop buckets. Removing his stocking cap, Jonny stuffed it into his pocket and shed his coat. As he tucked the coat between the bars of the tier gate, he realized that he was already sweating.

They went to the end of the tier with their mops and began to work back, swabbing the floor side by side. The tiers in this building were much wider than the narrow walkways in the cell-house they lived in. The floor was different too. Not dingy, crack-ridden concrete, but granite terrazzo. Jonny pressed down into it through the mop and concentrated on what he was doing.

"Holy shit," Seth murmured, pulling up.

Jonny ceased mopping as well and followed the young prisoner's line of sight. A huge cockroach plodded down the tier behind them.

"Jesus Christ."

Jonny was astounded by its size, which seemed

nearly pre-historic in proportion. Even by Walla Walla standards it was a giant. He wondered how he had missed it with the broom. Then he realized that there was no way he could have: this monster had wandered out of one of the cells.

"Go around him," Jonny said, returning his attention to the mop.

Seth did not argue—he had been around Jonny long enough to know his quirks. He mopped around the enormous bug and continued on his way.

When they finished mopping, Jonny went to the laundry room off the corridor and retrieved a stack of rags. Before leaving, he turned to the mountain of dirty linen bundled inside of sheets and stacked at the back of the large room. The smell of urine rose above a myriad of other odors. It took a lot of piss to smell that bad, he thought. He wondered if that was what would happen to him when he got old, that he would piss his own bunk.

Outside the room, he was relieved to again breathe air that was merely filled with dust. When he returned to the tier, he saw that Seth was not alone. The cellblock porter was with him—a hulking, bearded figure named Cowboy. Jonny wondered how he had talked O'Leary into letting him out of his cell. As he drew near, Jonny could hear what Cowboy was saying.

"I was in charge of the janitor crew at the Reformatory..."

"Here," Jonny said, stepping between them as he handed the rags to Seth. "Hit whatever's still wet with those."

"Jonny!" Cowboy greeted him as if he were his friend.

The porter's smile reminded Jonny of a crocodile's. Wide and impressive, but not supported by even a trace of goodwill.

"Did you ask Marks about getting me on the crew?"

"He says you're on his list."

Jonny turned and began to push one of the mop

buckets toward the utility room. He was disappointed in himself because he knew that he should have told Cowboy the truth. He had not talked to Mr. Marks about hiring him and, in fact, never would because he was the last person he wanted to be stuck working with. And he was conscious of why he did not tell him. Although they were about the same age, Cowboy was much bigger than Jonny. In fact, at six feet three inches tall and 275 pounds, he was bigger than most prisoners and fond of pointing it out. Although Jonny had never seen him fight, he had seen him bench press 500 pounds and easily rep the same amount for dead lifts.

In the utility room, Jonny poured the dirty water from the mop bucket into a floor basin.

"I'm tired of him saying I'm on his list."

The voice came from behind Jonny. He realized that Cowboy had followed him. Biting his lip, he took his time rinsing the bucket.

"I'm sure he'll call you soon," Jonny said finally, as he set the bucket down and attached a wringer to it.

Jonny tried to think of what he could say that would make Cowboy go away. Unscrewing the cap from a carton of floor finish, he hefted the heavy carton up from the floor and poured its milky contents into the mop bucket.

"It isn't Marks who picks who's on the crew anyway," Cowboy told him. "Your crew boss does it. And you know it."

Jonny tossed the empty carton away and looked directly at the thickly muscled porter. "All I know is that it's not up to me."

Cowboy's face darkened and Jonny instinctively shifted his weight onto the balls of his feet. Cowboy left without saying anything further. Jonny began to breathe easier.

"It's dry," Seth said, as Jonny wheeled the bucket back onto the tier.

"Let's do it then."

Jonny started at the front of the tier and worked backward, concentrating on laying an even coat of finish with the mop.

"He's not going to be on our crew, is he?" Seth asked behind him.

"No."

"He said he is."

"Who the fuck cares what he says?" Jonny snapped, as anger flared up inside him.

"I'm just telling you what he said." The younger prisoner sounded hurt.

Jonny turned his attention back to what he was doing, resolved to say nothing further about it. Each time he dipped the mop and tamped out the excess finish, Seth pulled the bucket further down the tier so Jonny could lay another section. Jonny covered all but the last 10 feet of the 200-foot tier with a glossy coat. He and Seth would wait there until the floor was dry enough for them to walk on again and they could move to the next tier.

Jonny set the mop in the bucket and walked over to a raised concrete step that extended out several feet in front of the last five cells on the tier. He sat down on it, and Seth did the same a few feet away, the young prisoner pulling his t-shirt up over his nose in an attempt to mitigate the smell of ammonia coming from the wet finish. It was overpowering in the unmoving air, although it had no affect on Jonny. He was used to it.

"Why'd they put this step here?" Seth asked. "It don't make no sense. It's only on the end of the tiers."

"Boxcars," Jonny told him.

"What?"

"Boxcars—you know, blackout cells. They built this cell-house originally to be the Hole, and the last five cells on each tier were enclosed in steel that extended out onto this step. When they slid the steel door closed on one of these cells it shut out all light. If you were in one, you couldn't see anything."

"Damn." Seth let the t-shirt drop from his nose, the ammonia smell forgotten. "You ever been in one?"

"They stopped using them before I got here," Jonny said. "They didn't need them after they built the IMU. I know a guy who spent a year in one though."

"Damn," Seth repeated, shaking his head. "I can't imagine, it must have been hell. I don't think I could do it."

"You could," Jonny assured him. "Besides, it's not like you would have had a choice."

"Well, I'm glad they don't do it anymore, so I don't have to find out."

"Hmph," Jonny snorted. "Things aren't any easier now. They might be different, but they aren't easier."

"What do you mean?"

Images of what Jonny had seen and experienced in IMU came back in a rush. Freezing strip-cells where prisoners lived naked. The bars that guards chained prisoners to in a standing position for twenty-four-hour periods, or longer. The prisoners he had seen chained, leashed, and beaten, then violated rectally under the pretense of a search. The pink underwear guards made them wear afterward. And the cell lights that were never turned off. Jonny could not bring himself to tell Seth about these things. He did not want to tell anyone.

"You haven't been in long enough to know," Jonny said, finally. "You'll find out."

"You ever been up to the gallows?" Seth asked, changing the subject.

Jonny shook his head. "No."

It was not the truth, but Jonny did not admit that to anyone. He had been up the stairs to the Death House. It was in the company of a sergeant who ordered him to push a cartload of fort-five-pound iron plates they had taken from the gym. It was not until they reached the stairs that Jonny realized what the weight was for: simulating the weight of a body in a test run of the gallows a week before a scheduled execution. He felt ashamed that he carried the weights up the stairs—no different than if he had allowed himself to be pressured into ratting someone out, or in some other way had violated the convict code. And a week after he did it, he also felt complicit in the act prison officials carried out.

"They tried to give Brady the death penalty," Seth said, as he stared at the floor.

Jonny was no longer listening to the young prisoner. His attention had turned toward the other end of the tier where Anton and Cowboy had come into view. Even at that distance, he could see that Cowboy was riding Anton's ear about something.

"C'mon," Jonny said, rousing Seth from his thoughts and getting to his feet. He laid a coat of finish over the final ten feet of the tier and headed off.

"Jonny, you tell anyone that I do the hiring for the shop?"

Jonny stopped short, anger rising inside him. He realized what Cowboy must have said. Jonny began to say something when Anton stopped him with a look. He realized that his crew leader had not asked something he did not already know the answer to.

Cowboy smiled and turned to Anton. "All I'm saying is, I don't see nothing wrong with a white motherfucker needing a job. Why not dump the toad and get me on instead?"

Jonny caught the subtle change in Anton's expression, although he doubted Cowboy did. He knew it would not have mattered anyway because Cowboy did not know Anton well enough to interpret it, to understand the line he had crossed.

"Is the laundry room open?" Anton directed the question to Jonny. Feeling his heart beating in the center of his chest, Jonny nodded.

Anton started down the corridor. Frowning, Cowboy looked at Jonny. But Jonny remained silent, his face impassive. He knew that he could not help Cowboy now even if he wanted to, which he did not. Cowboy headed off after Anton.

Jonny looked at Seth, who eyed him curiously. He realized the young prisoner was sharp enough to know that something more than the words exchanged portended what was happening, but he had not been around long enough to know what it was.

"C'mon," Jonny told him, leaving the mop bucket at the end of the tier and starting after Cowboy.

Jonny saw Anton turn off the corridor ahead of them and enter the laundry room, Cowboy behind him. He reached the doorway just as their crew leader attacked. Cowboy raised his hands in an attempt to protect himself, but it did not help. Anton landed three hard punches to his face that staggered him and knocked him backward.

"Why'd you do that?"

Cowboy's words struck Jonny as comical. The tough guy image he strove to project suddenly no longer there. A line of blood ran from his split lip.

Anton launched himself forward again with a leaping-type step that ended in a rapid barrage of punches. Jonny felt Seth press in behind him as he watched Cowboy back away and try to avoid the worst of it.

"Keep point," Jonny snapped, pushing the young prisoner back.

Jonny's eyes remained on the fight, watching for any sign that Cowboy might gain the upper hand. If that happened, he would jump in on Anton's side. The bearded idiot outweighed his crew leader by at least fifty pounds, but, up to this point, that did not seem to be a factor.

Cowboy made a brief attempt to hold his ground and fight back, but this only made it worse for him. He took another hard shot to the lips and again tried to cover up. Anton knocked one of the porter's thick arms aside and made him pay.

"Jonny."

Jonny turned, sensing panic in Seth's whisper.

"Guard." The young prisoner only mouthed the word this time.

Jonny pulled Seth into the room, then stepped out quickly into the corridor. O'Leary strolled toward him whistling quietly with his head down, as was his habit.

"Corky, don't come down here."

The guard stopped thirty feet away and looked up, his lips still pursed to whistle but sound no longer coming out. Several long seconds passed as both Jonny and the guard remained frozen, staring at each other, neither saying anything. The sound of heavy thumps, growls, and scuffling emanated from the laundry room.

Jonny shook his head, his composed exterior belying what he felt inside. The guard still did not move. But neither did the hand that had gone instinctively to his radio and now hung poised over its alarm button. That was where Jonny's attention was centered, the point upon which he knew his, Seth's, and Anton's immediate future hinged.

Finally, after what seemed a lifetime to Jonny, the guard's hand retreated back to his side. "You're right, I think I forgot something."

The guard forced a smile and nodded to Jonny. Turning back in the direction he had come, he set off down the corridor, whistling again with his head down.

Jonny breathed out in relief, suddenly cognizant that he had been holding his breath. Gratitude and newfound respect for O'Leary flooded through him.

"Okay—okay—okay!"

The words spilled from Cowboy just as Jonny stepped back into the laundry room. The burly porter was crouched over in a corner holding his hands out.

"Please...no more..." he pleaded between gasping breaths that hitched in and out of his lungs like sobs.

Slapping the hands aside, Anton stepped in and delivered a jarring punch to the side of Cowboy's head that knocked him down. Finally. Until this point, Jonny had not even been sure that Cowboy could be knocked down. He had taken so much punishment without faltering.

A second after the idiot thumped down hard onto his back, he managed to pull himself up into a sitting position, a look of confusion on his lumped face. Blood running from his nostrils and mouth had soaked into his beard and spread a sopping red stain down the front of his t-shirt.

Jonny checked the urge to run over to him and deliver a bootclad foot to his face. It was not because he did not want to that he did not. Deference for Anton prevented him. What happened next was his call, not Jonny's.

As Cowboy struggled to get to his feet, Anton looped an arm around his neck from the front and locked in a choke. The bully tried to extricate himself from the hold, but Anton only squeezed harder, forcing his head down and levering the sharp edge of his forearm against Cowboy's carotid.

Jonny felt Seth's hand on his shoulder.

"He's going to kill him." Panic had again entered the young prisoner's voice.

Jonny shrugged the hand off. He was not concerned, because he knew exactly what Anton was doing. It was not the first time he had seen him do this.

Cowboy's arms fell limp to his sides. And, for several seconds, all that maintained him upright was the hold Anton had on his neck. When he released it, the porter's body dropped like a sack of garbage.

Seth winced at the sound of his head striking the concrete. Anton hardly looked out of breath. He turned to Jonny. "You want to do it?"

Jonny knew Anton's words contained more than a question. There was also expectation in them. The punishment doled out to Cowboy thus far was not enough. He had gone out of his way to create a problem. One that could have ended with all of them being fired and thrown into the Hole. More had to be extracted from him for that.

Anton went to the door as Jonny approached Cowboy. Looking down at the unconscious form, Jonny contemplated stomping him out. It was the sanction most commonly meted out in situations such as this. Its purpose: to head off any inclination to pursue further what had already been dealt with. But, recalling Cowboy's ineffectiveness in defending himself and his pathetic plea for Anton to stop, Jonny did not believe that he would have the heart to start anything in the future. Not with their crew at least. On the other hand, he thought about how much he disliked Cowboy, how much he detested any bully. In fact, as Jonny stared down at him, he realized that it was not even Cowboy he was thinking about anymore. It was Eric Clayton.

Lifting a foot over the prone form, Jonny set it down on the other side, positioning himself directly above and astride Cowboy. Unfastening the front of his pants, he pulled out his dick.

"What are you doing?"

Jonny ignored Seth, who still sounded panicked. He focused instead on relaxing the necessary muscles. A second later, he began to piss. He was impressed with the flow, the coffee he drank earlier had done its job. Splashing across Cowboy's t-shirt, he adjusted his aim and began to wash the bully's face with the stream.

"Oh—sh-h-hit."

Jonny no longer even heard Seth. He was surprised at how easily the blood came off Cowboy. Pissing on his busted lips, Jonny had no doubt what the first thing the bully would taste when he woke up would be. The thought of that—Cowboy waking up—made him try to expedite what he was doing. It was not that he was afraid of Cowboy, because he wasn't. Well, less than before anyway. What concerned him was that his pecker was out. If he had to deal with someone, so be it. But he would rather it be when his junk was put away.

When the flow finally subsided, Jonny shook off

hurriedly and turned to leave. He saw that Anton was no longer there, and Seth stood frozen, staring at him, a look of disbelief on his face.

"C'mon, let's go," Jonny said, starting the young prisoner moving with a push. He closed the door behind them as he left the room.

They did not speak for a while. Collecting everything they had used on the first tier, they moved it to the other side of the cellblock and set to work on another tier. Jonny was about to begin laying finish when he turned to Seth.

"You want to give it a shot?"

The young prisoner was surprised. Applying the finish was a skill that had to be acquired and no one had offered to let him do it before. Jonny watched as he used the mop and was quickly impressed. The young prisoner moved it well, laying a smooth, even coat and leaving no *holidays*. He mirrored what he had so many times seen Jonny do.

"Hold up here," Jonny told him when they drew within a dozen feet of the end of the tier. "Not bad," Jonny acknowledged, as Seth set the mop back in the bucket.

Jonny had liked the young prisoner's work ethic and ability ever since he had first come to work with them. He was always willing to exert himself. And even when something was difficult for him at first, he picked it up quickly. Jonny wondered what he would have become in the freeworld if he had not gotten into the trouble that had got him sent to prison. He imagined that the young prisoner would have been able to do just about anything. As he sat down on the raised step at the back of the tier, Jonny thought it was most likely that Seth would have become a fisherman. Either that, or he would have joined the army. That was all there was in the corner of the state he was from. And not even that when the economy was bad and the government did not need anyone to feed to a war.

"Anton beat that guy's ass," Seth commented with a measured casualness. He sat a few feet from Jonny, not sure whether it was okay to talk about the fight or not. This was his way of testing the water.

"He can sling 'em," Jonny said, not volunteering any more.

What he did not tell Seth was that a number of times he had seen Anton fight and beat prisoners who, previously, he would not have believed could be beaten. Nor that he often mused about what he would do, how he would act, if he were able to fight as well as their crew leader. If he would have had the ability to fight like him before he came to prison, he would not have ended up there.

"He did not even say anything," Seth said. "He just gunned him down."

"What would you suggest he say? When it gets to that point, there isn't anything left to talk about. You do what you have to do."

A crease appeared on Seth's brow. "Jonny?"

"What?"

"I haven't been in many fights."

"So?"

"Well, I don't know how good I'll do if I got to get into it with somebody."

"Don't worry about it. When the time comes, you'll be all right."

Seth's brow retained the furrow. "Jonny?"

"Hmm."

"If I ever get knocked out, I hope no one does what you..."

Jonny began to laugh. Only a chuckle at first, then more. Unsure how else to respond, Seth laughed with him. One laugh genuine and full. The other empty and uncomfortable.

When Jonny checked the floor, he found it dry enough to walk on. Seth laid a coat of finish on the end of the tier and they departed. They had nearly made it off the tier when Jonny heard someone say his name.

"John."

"What's up, Mr. Brown?" Jonny greeted the old man standing at the bars of Cell #2.

Jonny noted how neat the five-by-eight-foot cell was. An old state blanket was pulled tight on the bunk and nothing was out of place. At the back of the cell, ghosts flitted silently across the snowy screen of a small black and white television. It struck Jonny that he could not remember a time when he had seen the set turned off, nor could he recall ever seeing Mr. Brown watch it.

The old man was wearing a stocking cap and state-issue coat. The coat's buttons fastened to the top and the cap rolled up at its edges in the manner peculiar to many old men. If Jonny did not know better—if he had not known that Mr. Brown at all times, no matter what the temperature or time of year, dressed this way—he would have believed he was about to go somewhere.

"Will you see Riff Raff today?" The old man asked in a voice as withered as he was.

"I can stop by his house," Jonny said.

The old man held up three packs of tobacco. "Will you take these to him?"

"Sure."

The old man produced another pack from his coat pocket and added it to the others before holding them out with knotted, trembling hands.

"You don't have to give me anything, Mr. Brown."

"Take it," the old man insisted, continuing to hold them out. "I know about your little business. You deserve it, go ahead."

"Thank you," Jonny said, taking the tobacco. He handed two packs to Seth and pocketed the remaining two himself.

"Anything else?"

"Here." The old man extended a hand through the bars.

"Thank you," Jonny said again, this time smiling as the old man dropped a handful of candy into his hand.

Jonny split the candy with Seth as they left the tier.

"How long has he been in?" Seth asked, still thinking about the old man.

"Maybe a nickel," Jonny said as he rinsed the mop bucket in the utility room. "He's got plenty more to go."

"What'd he do?"

"He shot his daughter's old man." Jonny paused. "Well, actually, he blew his head off with a shotgun."

Seth's eyes widened. "Why?"

"The guy used to knock her around a bit, I guess. Unfortunately for him, Mr. Brown is her father. From what I hear, he warned the guy, but..." Jonny shrugged. "I guess he thought the old man wasn't anyone he needed to listen to."

Seth shook his head. "That's fucked up. But at least he's not young. If you're going to get sent to prison, I think that's the time to do it, when you're old and have already done everything you wanted to do. It don't matter if they give you 50 years or a 100—they can't make you do it because you won't live that long."

It was Jonny's turn to shake his head. "It isn't like you think—it's harder for old guys like that," he said, setting the mop bucket on the floor and turning to look at Seth.

"Look at us," he continued. "We don't have nothing—and it isn't a big deal because we never did have anything. You came in young, like me. When you've been in as long as I have, you won't even remember what it was like outside prison. Not really. It'll be like a dream you had a long time ago but can't remember that good. And the longer you live here, the harder it'll be to remember and the less real it will seem. One day you're going to wake up and realize it's like this is all there has ever been in your life, you don't know anything else."

Jonny paused, as if to gather his thoughts. A moment later, he began to speak again.

"Mr. Brown had a wife and a house—and a daughter he obviously cared about very much. Those are things I don't think a man can ever forget, no matter how long he is in. I bet it would have been easy for him to stay comfortable out there, to continue to live his nice life, and not do anything to that guy. But he didn't. Mr. Brown did what he felt he had to do, despite knowing the state would make him die for it right back there in that piece-of-shit little cell, away from everything he loves. Getting sent to the joint when you're young, that's easy. You don't really even think about it—it's just something that happens. But getting sent here when you're like Mr. Brown—weighing all the options and deciding that despite the consequence it is what you have to do—I don't think that's easy at all."

They left the bucket and mops they had used outside the freight elevator, where Kevin would pick them up on his way out with the cart. Leaving the cell-house, they stepped out into a swirl of freezing wind in the courtyard. Jonny saw only a few prisoners out on the prison's walkways. And, like he and Seth, none of them were wasting time getting where they were going.

When they made it back to the shop, Mr. Marks was waiting for them with the equipment inventory in his hand.

"Where's the pressure washer?"

"The hospital," Jonny answered, hoping his supervisor would let it go at that, but knowing he would not.

"Who?"

Jonny hesitated, the way any good convict does when pressed for information, especially a name.

"Sgt. Ball," he said, finally.

"You let him take it?" It was an accusation posed as a question.

"What was I going to do?"

Mr. Marks frowned, relinquishing some of the tension from his face. Jonny had him on that and he knew it. Crossing to his office, he went inside and closed the door.

Jonny knew the hospital sergeant was, no doubt, about to receive a phone call. He only hoped that Mr. Marks did not mention his name. Sgt. Ball was a vindictive bastard, and life was not easy for anyone who got on his shit list. Especially if they were a prisoner.

"Grab a couple gallons of glass cleaner out of the back," Jonny directed Seth, who had settled on one of the milk crates beside the heater. When the young prisoner got up, Jonny went into the bathroom.

Seth was seated next to the heater again, a gallon of glass cleaner on either side of him, when Jonny came out of the bathroom. The young prisoner watched as Jonny plucked a broom from beneath his coat.

"What is that?"

Jonny ignored him as he slid the shank into the center of the straw bundle and wedged it in place. Holding the broom up, he inspected it. There was no way to tell the knife was inside.

Jonny glanced at the clock above the coffeepot. "Ready?" Seth reached for the containers of glass cleaner.

They did not make it far along the frozen street outside before Jonny began to feel anxiety well up inside him. He debated whether or not he should have brought the floor machine instead of the broom. There were places in a floor machine where a shank could be cached and would never be found. Smuggling it in the broom was risky. But he reminded himself of the time and suppressed his fear. He had enough time to do what he was doing. But not enough to change his mind about how he would do it.

As he entered Eight Wing, Jonny caught sight of Daugherty. The cell-house orderly locked eyes with him briefly before he disappeared around a corner. Jonny set the broom on the search table beside the metal detector and, as the guard inside the control station above him watched, both he and Seth passed through the device. Jonny picked up the broom on the other side.

"Did you two go through the detector?"

Jonny looked at the guard, who had appeared from around the same corner Daugherty had slunk around less than a minute earlier. The likely connection between these two events did not escape Jonny.

"Yeah, we cleared it. He saw us," Jonny said, pointing up at the control station.

"Do it again."

The guard's tone was hard, and Jonny felt a flame of anger spring up inside him, although he was careful not to allow it to reflect on his face because he knew it would only make the situation worse. Setting the broom back on the search table, he walked around the machine, mitigating what he felt for the guard with the knowledge that, at least, it was not Nieukoot. His shift had ended an hour earlier. Jonny again passed through the detector without setting it off, and Seth followed close behind him.

"Stand for search."

Jonny and Seth turned their backs and held out their arms. Pat-searching Seth first, the guard stopped at his coat pockets and pulled the packs of tobacco from them. He did the same to Jonny.

"You guys delivering these?"

"No." Jonny spoke for both of them.

"Hmph." The guard shrugged and slid the packs into a cargo pocket of his uniform pants. Any other time, Jonny would not let it go that easy. The guard had no right to take the tobacco from them. But Jonny could not afford a commotion, so he held his tongue. Picking up the broom, he turned to leave.

"Hold up, let me see that."

Jonny felt his heart leap into his throat and he froze. He realized that he had made a mistake not to argue about the tobacco. The guard expected it and, because Jonny had not, he sensed something was not right.

Jonny fought back an impulse to run. There was

nowhere for him to go anyway. He knew the guard in the control station would activate the electronic lock on the front door of the cell-house before he could reach it. Controlling his breath and maintaining a prison face, he turned and held out the broom.

Jonny's legs quavered as the guard took the broom. It was the same feeling he had in them the day they let him out of IMU. For him, at that moment, only two people existed in the entire world—himself and the unfriendly guard in front of him.

The guard eyed the broom with suspicion. Examining first one side, then turning it over, he examined the other. Jonny wondered how he did not feel how heavy it was. Twice the weight it should be. All he had to do was give it a shake and Jonny would be sunk. Perhaps not even that. It was possible the shank had already worked its way loose and was on the verge of falling out. An image of that came into Jonny's mind—the shank falling onto the floor between them. He knew that he would not be able to survive this time. Not another placement in IMU.

"Hmph." The guard shrugged again and lost interest in the broom. He handed it back to Jonny.

As Jonny took possession, a wave of relief washed over him and, although it did not reflect on his face, it spilled out of his mouth.

"Thank you."

Even as he said it, he realized it was dumb thing to say. What the hell was he thanking him for? Jonny hoped that his words did not reignite the guard's suspicion.

"What about our tobacco?"

The guard's face twisted into a mirthless grin and his eyes bored into Seth, who was the one who had spoken. "You want to talk to the sergeant?"

Jonny grabbed the back of the young prisoner's coat and pulled him with him as he walked away. The tobacco was a loss he was willing to accept. Debt was a better outcome than what could have happened. He would find a way to pay Riff Raff back.

Passing the shower room, they came to a door set flush into the old brick of the cell-house. It was made of thick steel plate, and Jonny was only able to raise a muted thumping sound from it with his fist. He hoped Loco was inside so he could get rid of the shank. The last thing he wanted to do was try to pass by the guard at the front of the cell-house again with it. He was relieved to hear the sound of the bolt being unlatched on the other side of the door. Pulling the heavy door open wide enough to enter, he slipped into the laundry room.

Jonny looked around the room in order to be sure the crazy-looking Mexican who had let him in was the only one there. When he was satisfied that he was, Jonny slid the shank out of the broom and handed it over.

The Mexican's eyes lit up in his tattooed face. "Thank you, Yonny—thank you."

Jonny noted that, although Loco's ability to speak English had improved since he arrived in the prison several years earlier, he still could not pronounce his name. He wasted no more time than was necessary to make his retreat and rejoin Seth outside the door.

"What should we do with these?" Seth asked, holding up the jugs of glass cleaner he still carried.

"C'mon," Jonny said, taking one of the jugs from the young prisoner and heading in the direction of the supply room. He was conscious that he felt lighter after getting rid of the shank.

Jonny slid the cleaner onto a shelf in the supply room, not caring which shelf it was or what was supposed to be on it. The room was Daugherty's responsibility and, because of that, it made no difference to him whether things were in the right place or not. He delivered supplies to this cell-house every week and his practice was to simply dump everything there on the floor in that room. He didn't do it because he was lazy. He carefully stocked and organized every other cell-house supply room in the prison. It was just that, as far as Jonny was concerned, Daugherty could fuck himself, and he wanted him to know it.

"You can go back to the shop if you want," Jonny said, grabbing a dustmop from the corner of the room and steering it toward the door. "I got to tell Riff Raff what happened to his tobacco."

"Do we have to pay it back?" Seth asked, already knowing the answer.

"Don't worry about it," Jonny said, absolving the young prisoner of any liability for the debt. "It's my problem."

"I'll come with you," Seth said, feeling relief and guilt at the same time. Grabbing a dust mop for himself, he followed Jonny out of the room.

They were met by a wall of noise as they stepped onto one of the trash-strewn ground-floor tiers of the cell-house. It was loud, although not as loud as it would be later when everyone who worked during the day returned. This was a kind of restrained pandemonium out of which no single sound rose much over any other, but when combined created an incessant roar. And, like the sounds, there was no single prisoner, or group of prisoners, more to blame than any other for creating it. With this many people stacked atop each other in so confined a space, tier upon tier and cell atop cell, there was no way it would be anything but loud. Even if those inside the building were not prisoners, it would be no different.

Jonny was proud of the fact that he was able to live here unaffected by the noise, at one with it. He moved through it, lived in it, without allowing it to invade him, to infringe upon his psyche, despite whatever level it rose to. This meant something to him because he had seen it drive others over the edge. Some, after a significant period of time, found themselves broken after spending years in it. Others, in no time, soon after they arrived and were dumped out there off the chain bus.

But this noise was home to Jonny, as much a part of the cell-house as the worn brick and crumbling mortar it was comprised of, and as much a part of him as the scar on his belly. He had always believed that if a motherfucker was able to live there, then there were probably not too many places outside the Walls where he could not live.

He and Seth set to work sweeping trash with the dustmops. Or, more accurately, they began to push it to one side of the tier, the side farthest from the cell-fronts. Jonny did not care whether the tier was clean or not. It was not the day of the week that their crew was scheduled to do it. Besides, he knew that no sooner would they clear it then more garbage would be thrown out. The bottom tiers of this cell-house were always covered with garbage. As far as Jonny knew it had always been that way. It certainly had for as long as he had been there. He and Seth swept solely for the benefit of the guard in the control booth above them. As long as it looked like they were doing something, that there was a reason for them to be there, the guard would not order them off the tier.

Jonny noted that Seth was doing a good job behind him. The young prisoner pushed the garbage aside as though he really meant it, his face intent. Maybe even overdoing it, Jonny thought.

Jonny was glad he no longer lived on this tier. It was where they had put him when he first got there. And it was not the garbage that had bothered him most about it. At least not directly. It was the cockroaches. There were more on the bottom tiers than anywhere else.

Jonny thought about what he would say to Riff Raff. He supposed it would be best to just tell him what happened. Riff would probably understand. Jonny was not sure how he would repay what he owed him.

A page torn from a magazine caught Jonny's attention and he stopped and looked down at it. The glossy image of a woman in a swimsuit stared up at him from the dirty concrete floor. Perfect, he thought. Except where the page was rumpled at the top, marring a shoulder. And ripped at the bottom, severing a leg. The picture made him think of Lessman her womanhood pushing out against her guard pants. He felt a tug in his groin.

"Yo, cuz, what's up with 5-0?"

Jonny turned to see a young black prisoner standing at the bars of Cell #13. Three others were busy tattooing in the back of the cell. They were running two guns at once and the drone of the small electric motors, which was distinct from the other noise in the cellblock, would be enough to give them away if a guard were to walk onto the tier. Jonny guessed the prisoner at the bars to be about the same age as Seth. He was trying to keep point, but he was limited in what he could see because he was not using a peep mirror.

"No cops," Jonny told him. "They're all up front."

The black youth nodded. "Good lookin' out."

As Jonny moved off down the tier, he wondered how long the black prisoner had been there. He knew it could not have been long because the way he addressed him had been devoid of the tension and enmity that generally ruled relations between their races inside the prison. He did not yet know he was supposed to hate white people.

When Jonny came to the last cell on the tier, he was surprised to see that Riff Raff already had the duck moved in. He lay on an upper bunk reading a magazine. Riff was in the back of the cell working on a drawing. Jonny had often been impressed by Riff Raff's skill as an artist. Some of his pieces he thought were even better than Corey's, although he did not believe it was really fair to compare them because Riff Raff did landscapes, which was much different than the spider webs, skulls, and Old English letters that were the hallmarks of Corey's trade.

Jonny did not know Riff Raff's exact age, but he

guessed him to be somewhere near forty. And although he preferred to keep him at a distance, Jonny did not think of him as a bad guy. He was aware that there were prisoners who did, but that was true for anybody. Jonny had to admit that Riff was a bit hardcore, but in that place that was an attribute. It simply meant that he was able to do more than make it through the experience. He had become hardened to the point that prison was his preferred condition, a place in which all that he wanted was available.

When Seth reached the end of the tier and pulled up beside him, Jonny knocked on the bars with the handle of the dustmop.

"Jonny!" Riff Raff greeted him as he came to the front of the cell. Reaching through the bars, he shook hands with Jonny.

The older prisoner turned to Seth. "How are you doing, youngster? Jonny steering you right?"

Seth shrugged. "Yeah, I suppose."

"Listen to him," Riff Raff counseled, his expression turning serious. "If anyone knows how to do time, it's him. He grew up in this motherfucker."

Jonny saw that the duck had set aside the magazine and was staring down at them from where he lay on the upper bunk. He fought back the urge to tell him to turn the fuck around. The duck was in Riff Raff's *house*. He was no longer any of his business.

"I got pulled over on the way in."

"What'd they get?"

"Three boxes from Old Man Brown."

"You didn't have the youngster packing 'em?"

"They still would have got took." Riff Raff was quiet a moment.

"Who was it?"

"Some guard who don't usually work the cell-house."

"The one from the Hole?"

"Yeah."

"He's a bitch." The older prisoner's tone hardened. "When can you get me back?"

Jonny's lips pressed into a line. "Tomorrow, maybe. Next day at the latest."

"Where's he at now?"

"Who? The guard?"

"Yeah."

Jonny shrugged. "In the office the last we saw him."

"Any others floating around the block?"

Jonny stepped back and looked up, scanning the tiers above. He shook his head.

"Tell you what," the older prisoner said. "Stand point and we'll call it even. Fair?"

Jonny felt immediate relief at the prospect of ridding himself of the debt. He nodded.

A smile flashed across Riff Raff's face, and he retreated to the rear of the cell, where he turned up the volume on a small radio. Jonny could hear the static-laced jazz over the unwavering noise of the cellblock. Riff Raff turned to the duck.

"Get down."

An uncertain smile formed on the duck's face. Hesitating a moment, he slipped over the edge of the bunk and eased himself to the floor instead of simply jumping down like anyone else would have. He turned to face Riff Raff.

"Get 'em up."

"W-what?"

The duck stepped back, but his heel banged against a footlocker. There was no room for him to retreat. Riff Raff did not move. He reminded Jonny of a snake studying its prey. The duck tried to reassert the smile that, a moment earlier, had disappeared from his face, but he failed to resurrect even a semblance.

"I hope he beats the shit out of that rapo," Seth said, his voice edged with excitement.

Ignoring him, Jonny scanned the tiers again to make sure no guards had entered the block.

Riff Raff struck with a blur of movement. In this, too, he reminded Jonny of a snake. The back of his hand landed hard against the side of the duck's face, knocking him to the floor.

"I said get 'em up, bitch."

Jonny heard Seth snicker beside him.

"P-p-please..." the duck stammered, struggling to get his feet back under him. Jonny could already see the imprint of Riff Raff's hand on his face. The duck's eyes brimmed with tears.

Stepping in, Riff Raff slapped him again. This time with his palm. The duck saw it coming, but there was nothing he could do. The blow struck the other side of his face, snapping his head back and knocking him onto the lower bunk.

The duck began to cry and blood appeared at the entrance of one of his nostrils. He stayed down this time.

"Get off my bunk, bitch."

"P-please, I don't want to fight you," the duck pleaded, his voice breaking as he cowered on the bunk, his inflamed cheeks wet with tears.

"Get the fuck up."

The duck began to sob and a fresh rush of tears poured out as he rose from the bunk. Riff Raff stepped forward, and the duck shrank away from him, pressing himself up against the bunk. There was nowhere for him to go. Jonny noted that he and Riff Raff were nearly the same size.

"I don't want to fight," the duck whimpered, his voice a broken whisper. Riff Raff's expression softened and he smiled.

"You don't have to fight."

The older prisoner's tone was suddenly tranquil, reassuring. He leaned forward until his face was an inch from the duck's.

"Don't make no difference whether you do or you don't. You're going to get fucked in your ass either way."

"What?" The duck was aghast.

Jonny heard Seth draw in an audible gasp.

The duck's expression changed. Panic entered his eyes, and he tried to step around Riff Raff, which was what the older prisoner was waiting for. Grabbing hold of the duck, Riff Raff wrenched him off his feet and slammed him onto the cell floor, driving him down hard enough on the concrete that Jonny could feel the concussion of the impact outside the cell.

Jonny again quickly scanned the tiers. No guards.

The duck tried to get up, but Riff Raff planted a knee on either side of his chest and pinned him to the floor.

"Don't—please."

Riff Raff delivered two stiff punches to the duck's face.

"N-o-o-o..."

Desperation was in the duck's voice, which grew louder. In fact, too loud. Locking his hands around the duck's throat, Riff Raff cut it off.

Jonny looked around at the neighboring cellfronts. No one was at their bars or seemed to be taking notice of what was happening.

Watching the rapo claw helplessly at the hands on his throat, Jonny could see that he had no experience fighting. His arms looked soft, lacking any muscle tone. He wondered what kind of life the duck had in the free-world. Easy, no doubt. It was over now though, Jonny thought. From here on out, nothing was going to be easy for him.

When the duck verged on unconsciousness, Riff Raff eased the hold on his throat, setting off a fit of gagging, gasping, and coughing. Before he had fully recovered, Riff Raff moved to reapply the hold.

"Stop—please..."

Clamping down on the duck's throat, Riff Raff cut off his words. Leaning over him, he again moved his face close to the duck's.

"I'll kill you, punk. You understand that? I will fucking kill you."

Jonny doubted the duck even heard Riff Raff. His face, already crimson, had begun to turn purple and his eyes bulged. He ceased to claw at the hands on his throat.

Riff Raff again eased the hold. A second later, he released it altogether. The duck coughed weakly and pulled in air, each inhalation a hoarse rattle.

"You're going to shut the fuck up and do what I tell you," Riff Raff growled, still astride his victim. "Got it?"

Jonny saw the duck nod and, no sooner had he done so, Riff Raff slapped him, landing a clubbing blow to his face. The duck began to sob anew.

"Answer me, bitch. I asked if you got it."

"I do, I do, I do." The duck's response was pregnant with resignation, submission. Jonny shook his head. There was no doubt about it now. The prisoner beneath Riff Raff was a punk and, before the day was over, everyone in the prison would know it.

Riff Raff rose from the duck's chest and stood up.

"Get up, bitch." He kicked the rapo, hurrying him to his feet.

When the duck was up, Riff Raff turned him around roughly, shoving him forward over the lower bunk. The duck tried to rise up, but Riff Raff gripped the back of his neck from behind, forcing him to maintain the bent over position.

"Stay down, bitch, or I'll knock you the fuck out. Then we'll do this again when you wake up."

"Don't—please," the duck whimpered, breaking into a fresh fit of weeping, but desisting from any further attempt to pull out of the position. He turned his tear-streaked face toward the bars, his eyes locking with Jonny's as Riff Raff jerked down the back of his sweatpants.

"Help—please." The duck mouthed the words, no sound coming from him. Jonny felt Seth's hand grip his arm and he turned.

"This is bullshit, Jonny," the younger prisoner hissed.

Jonny saw also what the younger prisoner did not say, but which was there in his eyes glaring out like an accusation. He wanted Jonny to say or do something, to somehow stop what was happening.

The sound of tearing fabric came from the cell and Jonny checked the impulse to look. He pushed Seth's hand off his arm.

"You didn't have to come."

The young prisoner stared back at Jonny, his expression hardening in anger.

"Uhhhh!"

The pained groan came from the cell, and Jonny again braced himself against looking in its direction. He knew better, although Seth did not.

"Oh God," the young prisoner croaked, turning away again quickly. He remained unmoving for a moment, not saying anything.

Jonny wondered if he was trying to prevent the image of what he had seen from becoming set in his mind. He was wasting his time if he was, Jonny thought. Once shit like that was in there, there was nothing you could do to get rid of it. He shouldn't have looked.

When Seth moved again, it was to depart swiftly. Jonny watched as he left the tier, dragging the dust-mop behind him and not looking back. Even after he was gone, Jonny continued to stare in that direction, his eyes turned away from the cell. The sounds of the rape came to him, unmitigated by the static of the radio or the din of the cellblock. One sound unrelenting and distinct among the others—the rhythmic thump of flesh pounding against flesh again and again and again.

Jonny ground his teeth. He did not like this shit either, but it was simply the way things were in that place. What could he do about it? He was not the one who made prison the way it was. This would happen whether he was there or not. What did Seth want him to do?

Miss the opportunity to get out of debt?

Seth would have to find a way to harden the fuck up, Jonny thought. The youngster allowed nearly everything that happened there to upset him, and that was no way to do time. Jonny knew he himself was a survivor. The years he had spent behind bars were testament of it, proof. He knew Corey was as well. And Little Matt. Each of them had learned to make it in their own way. And he knew that in his own way, Riff Raff was making it in there too. Perhaps better than the rest of them.

A guard came into sight at the head of the tier and started down it, startling Jonny from his thoughts.

"*One time*," Jonny announced, making the mistake he had thus far so carefully avoided. He swore as he averted his eyes quickly, but it was too late. The image penetrated him.

He could still see it, Riff Raff pounding roughly into his new punk's ass from behind. He was stuck with it. Like everything else he had seen in that place, it was now a part of him. He shouldn't have looked.

"Almost got it," Riff Raff puffed breathlessly from inside the cell.

The thumping intensified over sobs that were suddenly muffled. Jonny held his position on the tier as long as he dared. The guard drew closer as he walked slowly past cellfronts looking inside.

"He's on me, Riff. Gotta' go," Jonny said, when the guard was within fifty feet.

Pushing off with the dust mop, Jonny set off down the tier without waiting for a response. That was it, he thought. No more could be expected from him than that. Debt paid.

"Five-o," Jonny said as he passed 13 House, setting off a scramble inside the cell.

A lightbulb thrown from the third tier exploded in front of the guard, who stepped back and looked up, trying to determine which cell it had come from. Jonny made use of the opportunity to pass by him. He wondered what the guard would see when he got to Riff Raff's cell. It made no difference to him, he realized. It was no longer his concern.

Jonny returned the dust mop to the supply room, along with a pile of trash from the tier, which he left in the center of the floor. A present for Daugherty. He patted his pockets to be sure nothing was in them before he stepped through the metal detector. It was his habit—a good one for a prison smuggler. He saw no guards, but he knew that would change instantly if the alarm on the detector sounded.

"Hey, Anderson."

Jonny turned to see the guard who had taken the tobacco standing in the doorway of the guard office.

The guard waved him over.

As Jonny approached, he wondered what the guard wanted and why he had used his name. He reminded himself that he no longer had the shank on him, so he had no reason to worry.

"Want your tobacco back?"

Jonny did not respond immediately. Of course he wanted it back. He saw the packets in the guard's hand and wondered what kind of game he would try to play with him.

Finally, Jonny shrugged, unwilling to commit to any words.

The guard handed over the packets, which disappeared quickly into Jonny's pockets. For the second time that day he thanked the guard.

As Jonny left the cell-house, he tried to make sense of it. Maybe the guard was not as much of an asshole as he had thought. He decided that was not it. The guard wanted him to feel like he owed him. He would be back, Jonny was sure of that. As long as he watched for it, he would be all right. No guard was going to play him that easily.

He found Seth seated on the cart outside the shop in the cold. The young prisoner turned away as Jonny approached.

"You need to lighten up."

"That wasn't right," Seth said, continuing not to look in his direction.

"Maybe you should have thought about what was right and what wasn't before you came here," Jonny suggested. "It's a little late to run around and try to dictate what it is now. In case you haven't noticed, nothing in here is right. This whole goddamn place and everything that happens here is wrong."

Jonny paused for a moment, allowing the words to sink in, then he continued.

"He's a rapo. Whatever happens to him, he's got it coming."

Seth turned, finally, and looked at Jonny. "That's how you deal with rapos? You rape them? It isn't about what he is, Jonny—it's about what we are. Is that what we are in here?"

"It would have been different if he fought back," Jonny said.

"What's that mean?" Seth snapped, pressing the issue. "If you don't fight back, or you don't fight good enough, it isn't rape?"

"Fuck him!" Jonny exploded. "You think someone could do that to you? Do you?" Seth shook his head.

"I didn't think so. That motherfucker's full grown. If he can't fight for himself, I don't feel sorry for him. He's a punk, and that's exactly what he deserves to be."

Seth fell silent, his expression thoughtful.

Jonny sat down next to him on the cart and sighed, his frozen breath whisked away by the wind. He kept his hands as deep in the pockets of his coat as they would go, his chin tucked into its collar. A steady line of prisoners filed out of the industries gate, and he watched as they trudged off in the direction of their cell-houses. Too tired to hurry, despite the cold.

"Maybe I think too much," Seth said, staring without expression out at the ice-covered street in front of them. "Maybe that's why shit bothers me. I see people in here and wonder if that's what I'll be like in twenty years. Earlier, when you were talking to Mr. Brown, I wondered if that's what I'll be like when I'm old. But after you told me about him, I knew it wasn't. I'll never have a wife out there, or a kid. So what does that leave? What's going to happen to me, Jonny? Riff Raff scares me, but not in the way you think. He scares me because he makes me wonder if someday I'll get so fucked up in here I'll end up like him."

Jonny did not say anything for some time. What could he say? Seth was right. There was no way to know what would happen to a person or what they would become after years in that place. He thought about something an older convict had told him years earlier when he had gotten out of IMU and was having trouble sorting things out in his own mind. It had helped him then, and he had thought about it many times since. It was why he had gotten mad at Kevin earlier for what he had told Seth about his sentence.

"You can't lose hope," Jonny said. "Sometimes things in here seem bad, but there's always hope it can get better. You don't know what's going to happen. Twenty years from now we might have a governor who will give you clemency. You can't lose sight of that. It's how to get through this. Some days are worse than others, but no matter how bad it gets, as long as you remember there's hope, you can get through it."

Seth remained quiet for a minute. Then he tried to speak.

"Sometimes I..." The young prisoner's voice broke before he could catch it, and he turned away.

Jonny felt an ice pick slide into his heart. He wondered why he couldn't just shut the fuck up. Who was he to give advice? He did not have fifty-three years. And even with the time he had, it had been hard enough. How could he pretend to know what it was like for Seth?

When Seth turned back, his face was composed.

Jonny avoided looking at him anyway. "Want a smoke?" Jonny pulled one of the packets of tobacco from his pocket.

"You got it back?"

Jonny chuckled and handed Seth a paper. They rolled cigarettes together quietly and lit them.

Drawing in, Jonny realized how much he liked to smoke in the cold. It seemed almost as if the tobacco had a different flavor. Somehow better. The only drawback was having to have a hand out of his pocket.

The door of the shop opened and Anton stepped out.

"I've been waiting for you guys. I had begun to think you weren't going to make it back."

"What's up?" Jonny asked, curious as to why Anton had waited for them.

"The Mexicans are going to move on the Blacks in the Yard tonight. Don't get caught up—it's not our beef." Jonny nodded to his crew leader and watched him depart. Stepping out onto the street, Anton headed in the direction of Eight Wing.

Jonny and Seth remained where they were, putting off the inevitable as long as they could. When the last prisoner filed out of the industries gate and the massive steel door slammed closed, they knew it was time to go. The closing of the gate meant that the license plate factory had been cleared for the day. If they did not leave now, the tower guard would get on his bullhorn and order them to do so.

"Let's go," Jonny said, pushing stiffly to his feet. He extended a hand to Seth and helped him up. In no hurry, they set off down the street.

Inside the cell-house, Jonny made his way up the stairs with Seth not far behind. He navigated around prisoners hurrying from one place to another as they finished whatever last-minute business they were conducting before they had to return to their cells for 4:00 P.M. count. Stepping onto his tier, Jonny was again met with pandemonium. Louder than earlier because everyone was back from work. As he moved through it, individual sounds came to him out of the chaos. Toilets flushing, the slap of a domino slamming down onto a footlocker, a wood table being scraped across a cell floor, and cell doors crashing closed.

He heard rap music and could even make out some of the words. Something about being a "nigga" in a white man's world. He reflected on that as he neared his cell. But he could not see it because it did not match his experience. The color of his skin had never gotten him anything. Unless, nigga was an allusion to more than just skin color. If it was, he had no doubt that he was a nigga. The young prisoner behind him too, that was for goddamn sure.

Reaching his cell, Jonny opened the sign with the cell number on it. Through the bars he saw Matt hunched over a laundry bucket at the back of the cell, water sloshing out as he washed clothes. Corey lay on his bunk reading a newspaper. He was the only person Jonny knew who read all the sections. He did it every week.

The cell door jolted in its frame and slid open stiffly. Entering, Jonny unzipped his coat and shrugged it off as Seth followed him in. Hanging the coat on the corner post of his bunk, Jonny sat down atop a small wooden table next to Matt. Seth took a seat on the footlocker beside Corey's bunk, settling in to read the comics section Corey handed him.

Aware of Jonny's habits, Matt looked up at him. "Want to wash your hands?"

"It's not important."

Jonny noted the grease smears on his friend's arms and the tired look on his face.

"You'd think after a day in the slave factory, laundry would be the last thing on your mind."

"My dad and sister are coming this weekend," Matt said, as he worked soapy water into his clothes.

Getting down from the table, Jonny went over to another bucket in the corner of the cell and looked down. A small tangle of shredded paper lay on the bottom.

"Where is he?"

"He's in there," Corey assured him without looking up from the newspaper. "I put toilet paper in there so he'd have something to lay on, but he tore it up. I guess it's just what mice do."

Squatting beside the bucket, Jonny looked at the paper. He pushed the mound of torn pieces aside.

"What the hell? What did you do to him?"

The fur on the tiny animal stuck out in all directions as though charged with electricity. The mouse licked at it, trying to plaster it down, but his effort was to no avail. Squeezing in beside Jonny to look, Matt laughed when he saw it. Realizing the absurdity of the sight, Jonny did so as well. The mouse was a ball of fluff, its tiny nose and whiskers the only indications of which end its head was on.

"Dandruff shampoo," Corey explained. "It was the only way I could get that crap off." Reaching into the bucket, Jonny touched the animal warily with a finger, retreating as soon as he made contact. The mouse continued to groom himself, seeming not to be concerned.

Relaxing, Jonny began to pet him with his finger.

"You wouldn't catch me doing that," Matt said, shaking his head.

"I saved him," Jonny said. "I think he knows that."

"Ooooowwwww!"

Springing to his feet, Jonny shook his hand, trying to rid himself of the ball of puffed-out fur dangling from his finger by its teeth.

"Get him off!" Jonny yelled, his face contorted in pain as he held his hand out over the bucket.

Matt seemed unsure what to do. It was clear from the expression on his face that reaching out and grabbing hold of the rodent was not something he considered an option.

"C'mon!" Jonny urged. "Do something!"

Taking a pencil from a shelf, Matt used it to poke at the mouse, prodding it for nearly half a minute before it finally released its hold and dropped back into the bucket. It disappeared beneath the shredded paper.

Jonny swore as he pressed down on his wounded finger, shuffling his feet in pain as he tried to stem the flow of blood. Taking his towel from a hook near the sink, he wrapped it around his finger. He realized with a degree of annoyance that Seth was laughing at him.

"I didn't think that was a good idea," Matt said, returning to his washing.

"Danny's on his way back," Corey announced from behind the newspaper.

"McNeil?" Jonny asked, climbing back atop the table and keeping pressure on his wound with the threadbare towel.

"Yeah."

"Jesus, he was only out a month," Matt remarked.

"Twenty-six days," Jonny corrected, already having worked out the math in his head. Although Jonny knew an endless line of prisoners who had gotten out and come back, the news about Danny surprised him. He did not think he would be one. His friend had left determined to make it, to not come back. He and Jonny had talked many times about his plans to go to Alaska and get on a fishing crew, to work hard in the isolated environment of a fishing boat until he had enough money to return to Seattle and start his own business. He had wanted a tattoo shop. That was his goal when he left, his dream.

Danny's idea to fish in Alaska had come from an article he read in a *National Geographic*. Jonny realized that it probably was not smart to plan a future based solely on something you read in a magazine. But what alternative did they have in there? Inside the Walls, people learn how to live in prison, not out of it.

"They popped him on a couple of robb 1's," Corey

said, still reading the article.

"He'll get *all day* for that," Matt said, as he poured the soapy water from the laundry bucket into the toilet.

Jonny knew he was right. Danny was the same age as him and Matt, and a guy coming in at that age with armed robberies would be parked, maybe even struck-out.

Jonny remembered when Danny first came to the joint at nineteen years old for vehicular assault. He hit someone in a crosswalk after drinking at a party. He had not seemed to Jonny like the type to get sent to prison. But his beef, more than deliberate forms of street crime, defied categorization to any one type of person. It was possible for anyone to get drunk and decide that driving was a good idea. Whereas, a more narrow cross section of people found themselves inclined toward robbery. But it was the leap from one to the other that made Jonny pause for thought. How did a person go from hitting someone while driving drunk to armed robbery?

Jonny knew the answer. How could he not? It was all around him—the womb inside which they were warehoused, then spit back out into a society they no longer knew, nor that recognized them. The reproductive chamber of a malignant, stone-faced bitch who, despite how much her children avowed their hatred for her, was a mother who nurtured them in a manner that compelled them to return.

"I can't believe guys get out and come back," Matt said, echoing words Jonny had uttered many times himself. "Who in their right mind would come back to this? Just give me a chance..."

"It's not as easy as you think," Corey told them, lowering the newspaper. "Motherfuckers think that when they get out, they've made it. That's all there is to it. They think getting out is moving on to the promised land they've dreamed about all the years they were in this shit hole, the dream they've used to hold themselves together in here. The problem is, it's not that easy. You get out and find you don't know shit. Nothing is like you thought it would be, like you lied to yourself for years telling yourself it would be. People are running around everywhere out there and they know exactly what they're doing. And you don't know a goddamn thing. Think about it. All of a sudden you're out there in a world where everything costs money and you don't have nothing but the forty bucks they kicked you out with. Not even that, because they make you buy your bus ticket with it. Where are you going to stay? Even if you had money, it wouldn't do you no good because you don't know how to do nothing. Where are you going to work? When you fill out a job application, what are you going to put down for work history? You going to tell them that up until that point you've spent your whole life in the joint? Ain't no one going to hire you. And believe me, that's just the start of your problems out there."

Jonny remained quiet, thinking about what Corey had said. Corey was speaking from his own experience, which was why Jonny was unable to respond. He knew Matt could not either. Neither of them had ever been released from prison, nor even lived a day of their adult life on the other side of its walls.

"I'll tell you something else," Corey continued, looking directly at Jonny. "Some motherfuckers get released from IMU. Can you imagine that? Going straight from an IMU cell to the streets?"

Jonny, in fact, could not imagine it. He tried, but nothing was there. All he could relate it to was his own experience of being dumped back out into the regular prison after his stay in that place, which had been almost more than he could handle. Being thrown into the freeworld from there was inconceivable.

"Those are the guys who end up coming back for the hideous shit," Corey said. "Like Tank or Louie or Gangster. Think of one motherfucker that isn't true for. You can't. It's like prison broke something in them—fucked them up. Why would you do that to people—fuck them up, then release them into a world that operates under entirely different rules, a world full of people who have no idea what's being unleashed on them? The motherfuckers who run prison are either really stupid, or they want it to be exactly what it is—an industry that perpetuates itself."

"Brady was in IMU when they let him out," Seth said thoughtfully. "He did his last year and a half there."

Corey raised his eyebrows and again looked at Jonny.

"What about you?" Jonny asked. "You did pretty good. I mean, except for when you got busted."

"You got to have a plan before you get out," Corey said, warming to the subject. "And you got to keep it real, something you know you can make work. If you ain't real, you're fucked before you start."

Jonny looked beneath the towel at his finger, then covered it again.

"Last time I was in, I learned to cook dope," Corey continued. "I learned all I could about it and knew exactly what I was going to do before I left. Not everything worked out the way I planned, but that's where you got to improvise. If a motherfucker learns anything in here, it's how to do that."

"Did you ever think about getting a job and going straight after you bought the house?" Jonny asked.

Corey grimaced. "Where would I get a job? That was the best thing about cooking, I didn't have to rely on anyone but myself. I was my own job. Why would I want to do anything else?"

Jonny thought about what Corey was saying. Danny had left with a plan, but it was not practical. He thought about his friend, Pockets, in Six Wing, whose stretch would be up soon and who had already planned the robberies he was going to do when he got out. He was keeping it real, Jonny supposed. In his own way.

It was not what Jonny saw himself doing, though.

Despite what he was in prison for, the idea of running around and threatening people with a gun did not appeal to him. If there was a way to get out and make a quiet living, that was what he wanted to do.

"Will you teach me how to cook? I mean—before I get out, so I can be ready."

Corey frowned. "It's not as easy as just wanting to learn, there's a lot more to it than that." Jonny's hopes sank as Corey returned his attention to the newspaper. He considered pressing him, then decided against it. Better to catch him when he felt like talking about it, he thought. He would try again another time.

Jonny checked his finger as he slid off the table. It was no longer bleeding. He heard a pen click against a countboard and turned toward the bars. Three guards moved past the front of their cell. The last guard was the one who had returned the tobacco. He nodded to Jonny before moving on.

Stepping up onto his footlocker, Jonny launched himself onto his bunk. He found the automotive section of the newspaper waiting for him, and he managed to read most of it before the cell door clanked in its frame and began to grind open.

"E Tier! Mainline!"

The words blared from the loudspeaker, distorted to the point of being unintelligible. But everyone in the cellblock knew what was announced.

Peering over the side of the bunk to be sure Matt was not beneath him, Jonny swung his legs over and jumped down. Slipping past Corey, he grabbed his coat and pulled his boots out of where he had wedged them in the bars. Then he stepped out of the cell. As his cellies jockeyed around, getting in each other's way inside the cell, Jonny sat down on the tier and put on his boots.

Seth was next out and Jonny looked up at him as he tied his laces. The young prisoner had not taken his coat nor his shoes off over the count period. He never did. Probably why his feet smelled so bad, Jonny thought.

"You guys are going to get shut in there," Jonny warned as he pushed himself up onto his feet and put on his coat. He went a few yards down the tier and waited with Seth.

Corey came out of the cell wearing only one shoe and carrying the other in his hand. Matt exited behind him, fully dressed.

"Closing!"

The word barked from the loudspeaker as the long line of cell doors began to close. The sound of them slamming shut reverberated throughout the cellblock.

The four of them moved off down the tier and had nearly reached the grille gate at the front when Corey stopped.

"Goddamn it, my hat," he said, patting the empty pocket of his coat. He turned to go back.

"You won't make it."

Jonny's words stopped the big prisoner short. He realized Jonny was right. The guard in the booth would lock them all on the tier and they would miss chow. He decided it was not worth it.

When they reached the metal detector, another run of prisoners appeared at the top of the stairs and began to pour down. Seventy more bodies headed for the Chowhall. The crowd caught them at the front door and, as they stepped out into the cold, the prisoners in the lead began to pass them.

Jonny held to the same pace as his cellies. He was in no hurry. The Chowhall would still be there when they arrived and, it was just as certain, they would get no more than the allotted ration when they did. No point trying to get there faster. Besides, this was the way it was supposed to be done. It was smarter and safer to stick with your cellies. As long as you trusted them to have your back, that is.

The cold bit Jonny's face and stung his nostrils as he breathed in. The temperature had dropped since he and Seth had returned to the cell-house for count. Not that it rose much over the course of the day, but whatever moderation had taken place had left with the retreat of daylight from the now dark sky. Jonny found solace in the fact that the wind had stopped blowing. Burying his chin behind the collar of his coat, he pushed his hands deep into its pockets.

The courtyard was bathed in an eerie yellow luminescence from the stadium lights outside the Walls, which cast odd shadows inside. The kind of light that causes spots to appear in front of your eyes. Plumes of frozen steam rose from manhole covers along the course and tiny ice crystals floated in the still air, glittering in the light as they fell slowly to earth.

"It's cold as a muthafucka'."

The remark came from a black prisoner passing close on Jonny's right. Two others accompanied him. It was not what the prisoner said that caused Jonny to tense, but his proximity. He passed within inches. Too close. Seeing who it was, Jonny was not surprised. It was one of the prisoners who had been arguing on the tier earlier that morning. The loudest one. Jonny considered saying something to him. But as the three prisoners got further ahead, Jonny decided to leave it alone. The courtyard, directly under the gaze of Gun Tower #2, just was not a good place for it.

"You know what's for chow?" Matt asked.

Jonny realized he did not know. But he was hungry and knew that he would eat it no matter what it was. They all would, so it did not matter. He was about to tell Matt as much when another black prisoner moving past on their left caught his eye. He was alone and moving quickly. Too quickly. His attention was on the three prisoners now ten yards in front of them. Jonny noted how young he was. He looked younger than Seth.

Jonny turned and made eye contact with Corey, whose radar, he could see, had been tripped as well. The prisoner on their left was the other one involved in the argument that morning.

"Seth."

Jonny said his name just loud enough for his cellie to hear it. He had drifted several yards away, but when he heard Jonny, he pulled back into the group.

The three Blacks spotted the young prisoner before he reached them and they turned, causing him to pull up. The staggered line of prisoners headed to the Chowhall slowed as people realized that something was happening. The prisoner who had passed close to Jonny stepped forward and Jonny saw how much bigger and more solidly built he was than the younger prisoner. If he were to bet on this, Jonny knew that he would have to go against the youngster.

"What'chya wanna do, nigga? You grow a nutsack all a sudden?" The older prisoner raised his fists and squared off.

Jonny looked around and saw that other prisoners were crowding in around them, the confrontation blocking passage to the Chowhall. When he turned back, he saw the younger prisoner had also raised his fists.

"Knock his bitch ass out, T-Bone!"

The shout came from behind Jonny, and he saw the older prisoner smirk, seemingly emboldened by it. Apparently he was T-Bone. But Jonny also saw a look of determination form on the young prisoner's face. He was the one who charged first, throwing wild, looping punches as he rushed in.

Jonny felt bodies pressing in behind him as many in the crowd tried to get a better look. The electronic screech of the tower guard's bullhorn rose in the distance, but Jonny's attention remained fixed on the scene in front of him. The older prisoner stepped back in an attempt to evade the younger prisoner's attack. Jonny knew as soon as he was able to, the older prisoner would launch an attack of his own that would probably end the fight. Unfortunately for him, he did not last long enough. His foot slid from beneath him on the ice and he dropped his hands to catch himself. He paid for it with a hard right to the jaw that crumpled, him and he dropped onto the frozen concrete.

The young prisoner hesitated, staring down at his no longer conscious opponent in disbelief. Jonny felt like cheering for him.

"Hah!" The young prisoner ejaculated this as loud as he could, the sound of pent-up fear and tension finding sudden release. Stepping forward, he kicked the unmoving body.

It was a lame kick really, Jonny thought. He could see the young prisoner was more concerned with not losing his footing than causing damage. And Jonny understood that. After all, how would it look? To win a fight like he had, then fall on his ass in front of everyone.

The young prisoner stepped back and again shouted at the unconscious form. "Hah!"

Craaackkk!!!

The lethal-sounding report pierced the frozen stillness of the courtyard. The young prisoner dropped, his body landing splayed out and unmoving.

"They shot him," Seth murmured, incredulous.

Jonny ducked down at the sound of the shot and, as he began to straighten back up, the voice of the tower guard came over the bullhorn.

"Everyone down now! Get down!"

The voice was loud despite the distance. Jonny supposed it was because there was no other sound. Looking at the immobile form on the ice, he felt anger envelop his heart.

"They shot him," Seth repeated dumbly.

Jonny noted that everyone around them remained standing, no one complied with the order to get down. Suddenly another voice rose up in the courtyard. This one did not come over a bullhorn, but it was loud and carried.

"YOU FUCKIN' COWARD ASS P-I-I-I-I-G!"

Craaackkk!!!

Jonny ducked again, conscious that his reaction

was instinctive and served no real purpose. If the tower guard was aiming at him, he would be shot. Jonny wondered what he was shooting at.

"Everyone down! Last warning!"

It was the voice over the bullhorn again. This time Jonny sank to a squatting position and, beside him, Seth followed his lead. They heard Corey swear behind them as he and Matt lowered themselves as well. Every prisoner in the courtyard got down.

A half dozen guards burst out of the twin doors at the entrance of the Chowhall, two nearly falling as they lost their footing on the ice. They headed for the two unmoving prisoners. And more guards came after them, converging from other areas of the prison.

"On your bellies! Face down!"

A sergeant arriving on the scene yelled this. Jonny saw him push a Mexican prisoner down roughly as he passed. The other guards began to yell the same command.

Jonny swore under his breath. What was the point of making them lay out on the ice? He eased onto his belly, as did the other prisoners in the courtyard, because all of them knew that anyone who did not comply would be dragged to the Hole. That is, if they were not shot.

"Don't move."

The command came from a guard standing over the prisoner who had been knocked out. T-Bone was starting to stir, moving his head back and forth and groaning. He was already in handcuffs. Reaching down, the guard and another gripped the back of his coat and pulled him up from the ground. Two more guards joined them, one taking hold of the prisoner's cuffed wrists and levering them high behind his back.

"LEAVE HIM ALONE YOU PUNK MOTHERFUCKERS!"

The shout froze every guard in the courtyard, then they turned and looked over the swathe of prisoners laid out in the direction it had come. Jonny recognized the voice as the same he had heard earlier. The guards looked angry. Three started in that direction as the handcuffed prisoner was dragged away still not fully conscious.

Jonny's ears rang from the shots. He knew of no louder sound that he had ever heard inside the Walls than when a rifle was fired from a gun tower. It reminded him of the crack of a whip—but a hundred times louder.

Jonny saw Lt. Mason coming through the security gate, the outline of his 400-pound body unmistakable. He headed toward the prone form of the prisoner who had been shot. Hearing the jangle of keys, Jonny turned and saw the sergeant locking the doors of the Chowhall. He eyed the doors with regret, lamenting the fact that they had not made it inside. If they had stayed with the others from their tier, he knew they would not be out there on the ice like they were. They would be inside that building, eating and warm.

Jonny took an inventory of his extremities. He no longer felt his nose or fingers, and his toes were nearly as bad off. He wondered how long they would make them lay there.

"I should have gone back for my hat."

Jonny twisted sideways slowly, in order not to attract attention, and looked behind him at Corey. "Want mine?"

Corey shook his head.

Turning back around, Jonny saw that Lt. Mason was only thirty feet away. He had joined the cluster of guards standing over the prisoner who had been shot. Watching the obese lieutenant stare down at the unmoving form, Jonny wondered what he would order the guards to do.

"Medical's on the way," the lieutenant grumbled.

It was not clear to Jonny whether the lieutenant was speaking to the prisoner or the guards around him. Jonny noted that none of them had examined the young prisoner in order to try to determine the seriousness of his injury. Other than rolling him onto his belly and handcuffing him, they had not touched him. Jonny wondered if he was dead. He had not moved since he had dropped to the ice. Not even a tic. But the guards would not have handcuffed him if he was dead. Would they?

Jonny wondered what would happen if he were to get up to try to help the young prisoner. But he realized he already knew. Best-case scenario would be that guards would jump on him, ratchet cuffs onto his wrists, and haul him to the Hole. More likely, though, they would shoot him. Thinking about this made Jonny glad that it was not Corey, Seth, or Little Matt laying there. He wondered what was taking Medical so goddamn long.

Jonny watched the lieutenant prod the body with the toe of his boot and get no response. Wedging his boot beneath the body, the lieutenant turned it onto its side and Jonny stared hard trying to make out where the young prisoner had been shot. But it was impossible to tell in the yellow light.

Jonny again felt anger licking at his heart. He realized that it was in situations like this that it was most clear how these people felt about them. How they regarded them was never well disguised, and could always be felt to one degree or another, but it was at times like this when even the pretense of disguise was abandoned. To these people, they were not human beings. Less than animal even. They did not pack animals into zoos like they were packed into these cell-houses. And if animals were in overcrowded conditions, they were not shot when they got into a fight. The more Jonny thought about what was in front of him, the more it upset him. Guards stood over the young black prisoner as though he were a deer kill. They talked idly and joked between each other as they waited for Medical, which, Jonny had begun to suspect, might never show up.

The lieutenant pushed again at the body with the toe of his boot.

"GET YOUR STINKIN' FOOT OFF HIM YOU B-I-I-I-T-C-H-H-H!"

Jonny suppressed the urge to laugh aloud. He was too close to the guards for that. Whoever yelled had really got their attention this time. Guards set out immediately in the direction the voice had come from. This one pissed them off.

While the guards' attention was drawn to the other side of the courtyard, Jonny took advantage of it. After a quick glance at the gun tower 100 yards away, he shifted around slowly so that he could see Corey and Matt without having to turn.

"Here," Jonny said, pulling his cap off and passing it to Corey.

Corey nodded to him and stretched the cap over his head, pulling it down over his ears, which Jonny noted, had turned an angry red.

"You think he's dead?" Matt asked.

"He's dead," Corey said, avowing what he believed to be true. "When a motherfucker drops like that, they're dead."

Jonny nodded. He had to agree. Relating it to his own experience of being shot, he believed Corey was right. It was just not possible to take a bullet and be still or quiet. Unless, of course, you no longer had a choice.

"There they are," Seth said, alerting them to a sudden bustle of activity at the security gate.

Jonny saw a guard pull a gurney through the gate. As he set off across the ice, the gurney clattered and vibrated as if threatening to come apart. Behind it, a nurse struggled to keep up, and Lt. Todd strolled casually at his usual, unhurried pace. Jonny heard a number of prisoners grumble around him, although, he noted, none loud enough for Todd to hear.

The guards standing around the body parted and

made room for the nurse. Although she was old, Jonny had often wondered how long she had been a nurse, or even if she actually was one, because of things he had seen her do in the past. She looked down at the young prisoner on the ice as though she were not sure how to proceed. Bending down, she took hold of the sleeve of his prison-issue coat and tugged on it.

"Hey. Wake up."

The body did not move.

"C'mon now! Wake up!" The nurse said it louder this time, her voice carrying the rasp of a lifelong smoker.

Jonny wondered if what she was doing was proper emergency medical procedure. He doubted it.

Unable to elicit a response from the young prisoner, the nurse pushed up the sleeve of his coat and held one of his cuffed wrists. A moment later, her latex-gloved hand moved to the side of his neck.

Jonny noticed something that he believed he should have seen from the start because it was so obvious. Everyone's breath was frozen and visible, except for the black kid's. He had no breath.

The nurse looked at Lt. Todd and slowly stood back up. Slipping her hands into the pockets of her coat, she shook her head.

"You and you," the lieutenant said, pointing at a pair of guards standing near the gurney. "Get him out of here."

The guards charged with moving the body went to work. One took hold of the prisoner's feet, the other gripped a handful of coat at each shoulder. When the guard with the feet nodded, each of them lifted his end of the body and swung it onto the gurney. The black kid was still handcuffed and Jonny wondered what the sense was in that. One of the guards fastened a belt attached to the gurney across the middle of the body and cinched it. Jonny wondered how many times they had done this. They seemed good at it.

The courtyard was silent except for the clatter of the gurney as it was wheeled away across the ice. Jonny saw a dark stain on the ground where the body had been.

The two lieutenants assembled a group of six guards, and Jonny watched as Lt. Mason issued them a series of terse instructions before dismissing them with a wave of his gloved hand. Accompanied by the sergeant, they crossed to the far end of the courtyard and picked out three prisoners, who they ordered to get up. This was the area from which the shouting had come.

The guards split into pairs, each taking up position behind a prisoner and putting handcuffs on them. Jonny noted they had made an equal opportunity selection—a black, a white, and a Mexican. Their idea of fair.

"I no yell," the Mexican protested as the guards behind him pushed him forward. "*No es me.*"

The guards grabbed his arms and began to pull him along. Perhaps realizing that complaining about his fate would not accomplish anything other than loss of face for himself and his race in the eyes of the other prisoners, the Mexican fell silent and began to march in step with the guards. Every prisoner there knew that no matter what was said, these three were going to the Hole. The decision was already made, so there was no use trying to dispute it. Jonny doubted that any of them was the one who had yelled. It certainly was not the Mexican because his accent precluded it. But Jonny knew that whether they had done it or not was not the point. The point the guards were making was that it did not matter if they knew which specific prisoner had done it. Someone was going to the Hole for it.

"At least they don't have to freeze their asses off anymore," Corey muttered.

The words rang hollow. He knew as well as Jonny that what was happening to the three prisoners could in no way be interpreted as fortunate. It would be a long time before they would be seen in general population again.

When the three prisoners disappeared through the security gate, Lt. Todd struck out across the ice and came to a stop directly in front of Jonny and his cellies. Jonny did not look up at him. He did not want to draw attention to himself. All he was able to see were Todd's stiffly creased pant legs and shiny black boots less than five feet from his face. The scar on Jonny's lip itched.

Jonny wondered why Todd had stopped there. Had he seen them talking? Would he order that they be sent to the Hole too?

Several guards joined the lieutenant, awaiting his instruction as he stared at the prisoners laid out before him.

"All right, let's get them up and over there against the wall," Todd said, finally. "Slowly, a few at a time. And start here in the front."

The guards began allowing prisoners to get up six at a time and ordered them to line up against the side of the building that housed the Chowhall. Jonny and his cellies rose with the second group and took their place against the wall, thankful to be off the frozen ground. The more prisoners that got up without incident, the faster the guards proceeded. They ordered the last twenty up at the same time, and it was in that group more than fifty yards away that Jonny spotted a familiar coat. He realized that the prisoners in the courtyard were from Anton's tier, and Anton was among them.

Jonny's hands were in his coat pockets, but he was frozen through so thoroughly that this did not bring him any warmth. He wondered what the guards would do next. Would they just let them return to the cell-house, and that would be the end of it? He did not think so. Nothing in the joint was ever that easy.

Lt. Todd went into the cell-house, taking most of the guards from the courtyard with him. This left only Lt. Mason, the sergeant, and a handful of others outside to keep an eye on them. And they did not look happy about it.

The sergeant ordered all prisoners not to talk, then took up a position less than a dozen feet from Jonny, poring over the line with suspicion-laden eyes. He did not impress Jonny. Eyeing the sergeant, he took in his weak jawline and pronounced snout. A rat face, Jonny thought. He wondered what the sergeant did when he was not at the prison. He looked even less like he belonged outside the Walls than Tony No Fingers. Then again, what did Jonny know about the world outside the Walls?

Looking at the tower, Jonny saw there were two guards up there. Both with rifles pointed in their direction. A disturbing thought came to him. Perhaps they planned to shoot them. Maybe that was why Todd had ordered them lined up against the wall. They had witnessed a crime, and the guards felt they needed to cover it up.

Jonny caught himself. He wondered if it was the cold that had his imagination running out of control. The guards were not worried about witnesses because there had been no crime. It was not a crime to shoot a prisoner. No one would question why they had decided it was necessary to put a bullet into a lousy convict. This was their house, and they could shoot whoever they damn well wanted.

The front door of the cell-house opened and a guard stuck his head out. "Four at a time," he told Rat-Face and disappeared back into the building.

"Four!" The sergeant barked, holding up a corresponding number of gloved fingers.

Jonny supposed this was in case there was someone among them who did not know what the word *four* meant.

After the first group went into the cell-house, Jonny counted the prisoners in front of him. There were ten. Turning to Corey, he mouthed the word "search." Corey frowned and shook his head in disgust. Pulling the stocking cap from his head, he handed it back to Jonny, whose six-digit prison number was stamped inside.

Jonny considered letting a couple people go in front of him, so that he, Corey, Seth, and Matt would enter the cell-house in the same group. But, when he thought about it, he could see no benefit to be gained, so he held his place in line.

When it was Jonny and Seth's turn, they entered the building behind two other prisoners. Jonny saw that the front of the cell-house was crowded with guards, most of them standing around not doing anything. In the enclosed area it seemed like there were more than had been in the courtyard. Two pairs of guards wearing latex gloves and standing in front of the others hailed them.

"First two! Step up!"

Jonny and Seth remained by the door as the two prisoners ahead of them stepped forward, each in front of a set of guards. Lt. Todd stood behind the guards, his eye alert. Jonny had often thought his prison face was as good as any convict's. No different than the five-and-a-half-foot thick granite wall that surrounded the prison. From outside, there was no way to tell what was going on inside. The only thing you could be certain of was that it was not anything nice.

"C'mon, we don't have all day. Strip!"

Every guard in the cell-house watched as the two prisoners in front of Jonny and Seth began to undress. Five female guards stood together near the stairs registering varied expressions of contempt and disgust.

God, he hated this shit, Jonny thought. Stealing a glance at Seth, he saw that the young prisoner looked horrified. And Jonny understood his dismay, considering that he had not been through this before. The young prisoner did not like going down to the crowded shower room. He was definitely not going to like this.

As the prisoners stripped, they handed each clothing item they removed to the guards who looked it over, then dropped it on the floor. Jonny knew that it was not that what was happening disturbed him any less than it did Seth. It was simply that he had been through it before. Many times. There was no way to get through ten years of prison and not go through this experience, and a thousand others equally, if not more, disturbing. The truth is, it never gets easier. But, like anything else that happens in there, you have to find a way to deal with it. It is the only way to move forward.

Jonny was aware that his way of dealing with what the guards were doing was to shut himself down, that part of himself that was concerned with what others thought of him. The trick, he knew, was to tell himself that none of this mattered because he did not give a fuck what any of these people thought about him. Including the women. The trick was to derive strength from his prison face. To make those doing this to them, and himself, believe that this in no way bothered him. Indeed, he knew it was those the guards saw that it bothered that they gave the worst to.

When the two prisoners were completely undressed, standing barefoot and naked on the dirty concrete floor, Jonny could not help but notice that one was hairier than hell. A forest of dark hair covered every part of him, even his back and shoulders.

"All right, Wolf-Boy, open your mouth," One of the guards in front of the prisoner said, as he stepped forward to look inside the prisoner's mouth.

Several guards snickered nearby.

"Lift your tongue."

The prisoner complied.

"Okay," the guard said, taking a step back. "Arms."

The prisoner raised his arms so that his armpits were visible.

"Sack."

The prisoner reached down and lifted his scrotum.

"Turn around," the guard commanded.

The prisoner turned away and faced toward Jonny and Seth.

"Feet."

The prisoner lifted his feet one at a time, showing the guard their undersurface.

"All right, Wolf-Boy spread 'em."

The hairy prisoner bent forward and reached behind him to separate his buttocks. Jonny looked away while he was being made to assume the demeaning posture. After baring his anus to the guards, the prisoner straightened back up.

"Hold up," the guard said, shaking his head. "That don't cut it. You need to spread and hold until I tell you you're done. You understand?"

Jonny felt his body tense. This game was not an unfamiliar one. The guards played it often in IMU.

For several seconds the hairy prisoner did not move. He stood staring at the guard, his face tight with anger.

"You wanna refuse?"

The question was a threat.

The prisoner's shoulders slumped. And he again turned around.

This time Jonny did more than simply look away. He turned around completely, as if showing that he refused to watch could somehow help the prisoner this was happening to.

There was more snickering among the guards.

The anger Jonny felt burn in his heart brought resolve with it. He was not going to let them do that to him. He would not stand for it. If running through these motherfuckers' little dance of humiliation once was not good enough, then they could go ahead and take him to the Hole. Hell, he would go back to IMU before he let these punk bitches do that to him.

When the two prisoners moved to the side and began dressing, the guards ordered Jonny and Seth forward. Jonny did not look at them, he concentrated instead on what he was doing. His hands had no feeling in them from the cold, and he fumbled clumsily with his clothes as he removed them. The zipper on his prison-issue pants gave him the most trouble and, as he worked to get it down, he was beset by an anxiety that had not occurred to him until this point. He told himself again that none of what was happening mattered because he did not care what any of these people thought of him. But when he stripped off his underwear, what he saw beneath caused his face to flush with an unbidden warmth. His penis and testes had retracted from the cold and pulled in tight to his body. To say the least, it was not an impressive sight.

As the guard in front of him issued commands, Jonny went through the requisite motions. They were so ingrained in him that he did not even need to listen to what the guard was saying. Someone snickered when he was ordered to bend over, but he ignored it.

When he straightened back up and turned around, he was ready. If the guard told him what he had done was not good enough, he would go to the Hole.

"What happened to you?" The guard asked instead, as Jonny bent forward to pick up his clothes.

"What?" Jonny was not sure what he was talking about.

The guard nodded toward his midsection. "Someone stab you up?"

So that was it, Jonny thought. He wanted to know about the scar. But Jonny did not like to talk about it because he did not feel it was anyone's business but his own. He resented questions even when they came from other prisoners. The fact that this one came from a guard that had just done his best to humiliate him only made it worse.

"I was shot by a pig."

The guard's face tightened.

Jonny was conscious that all of the guards were watching, and that he was still naked. He wondered what they would do. Would they take him to the Hole now? He knew if they did, they would march him there just as he was. Without clothes. He realized that he did not care.

"Hmph," the guard snorted finally. "It didn't happen here, I can tell you that. We shoot better. But you probably already know that."

Guards all around them began to laugh. It would not have surprised Jonny if they had broken into a round of applause, they seemed that pleased with themselves. But he did not care about that either. Bending forward, he grabbed his undershorts from the pile of clothes on the floor and began to dress. He had said what he wanted to say, and he did not really give a damn what they said back. All he wanted to do was get away from them.

"Four more!" The guard bellowed while Jonny pulled on his boots.

Jonny left without tying them. He passed the group of female guards near the stairs, but avoided looking at them. He ascended the staircase as quickly as he could and waited for Seth at the top. Neither of them said anything as they walked back to the cell.

Inside the cell, Jonny retrieved the car magazine from beneath his bunk pad and took a seat on the end of his footlocker. Opening the magazine, he pretended to read. Seth climbed up onto his bunk and laid down.

Even if he wanted to, Jonny could not have concentrated on reading. Too many thoughts crowded into his mind, demanding to be sorted out. He knew from what he had heard from other prisoners over the years that there was a marked difference between how male and female prisoners were treated in the state. At the women's prison, male staff were not allowed to be present when female prisoners were strip searched. They were even barred from being in areas of the prison where the women might not be fully clothed. Yet it was all right to do this shit to them because they were men? Jonny did not understand that. It was not that he begrudged women prisoners the measure of dignity they were afforded. He simply could not see why they as men should be treated differently. If it was wrong to do this to women, it was wrong to do it to them as well.

When Jonny thought about it, though, he supposed the way they were treated made sense from the perspective of the people who ran the prison. Managing a group of people as if they were less than human, and actively fostering an attitude of contempt for them, undoubtedly made it easier to keep them in crowded, locked cages with sentences many would never live to see the end of. It certainly made it easy to shoot and kill them.

The cell door began to open. Leaning out, Jonny peered down the tier and was confounded to see Matt and Corey laughing as they approached. What was there to laugh at? Returning to his seat on the footlocker, Jonny again picked up the magazine.

"I can't believe you," Matt said, as he and Corey entered the cell. Sitting down on his bunk, Matt shrugged out of his coat.

"You should have been there, Jonny. They told us to strip out, and as soon as we got our clothes off, Corey over there blasted out a fart so loud it put the guards into shock. They didn't know what to do. They couldn't even say anything."

Jonny realized why they had returned laughing. He looked at Corey, who lay on his bunk with a self-satisfied smile on his face.

"Now they know what we have to deal with," Jonny said.

"I wanted to laugh," Matt continued. "But when I saw Lt. Todd's face, I didn't dare. He was pissed. I thought for sure he was going to do something fucked up to us. But that's when it hit them."

"What?" Jonny asked.

"The smell. Oh my God, it was horrible. I thought I was going to blow chunks right there."

Seth began to laugh, hard enough that he rocked back and forth on his bunk. Inhabiting the bunk above Corey, he knew better than anyone what Matt was talking about. There were nights that he had been jolted out of his sleep by a smell that hit him no less violently than if he had been slapped awake. On those occasions, he had no choice but to scramble down from his bunk as quick as he could and go to the bars at the front of the cell in order to gasp for air.

"You guys should have been there," Matt told them, shaking his head. "The guards tried to move away from us, but there was no getting away. It was everywhere. Todd yelled at us to pick up our shit and get the fuck out of there. They didn't let us get dressed until we got to the top of the stairs."

Jonny walked over to Corey's bunk and slapped five with his cellie's ham-sized hand. Suddenly, all of the doors on the tier racked open. Except for theirs.

Retrieving the peep mirror, Jonny went to the bars and held it out.

"They're running everyone back," he said, letting the others know what he saw. "They must have let them out of the Chowhall."

"Lock up! Lock up now!" The loudspeakers blared. "They're locking us down," Matt said.

"Fuck," Corey swore. "There goes our Yard-time."

Jonny remained at the bars, watching prisoners make their way back to their cells unhurriedly. Everyone knew that was where they would be stuck for the rest of the night.

No Yard was bad news. Jonny had been looking forward to getting some exercise. Especially since he had not made it to Yard the day before. Matt would not be able to run, which was how he usually spent his Yard-time, even when it was as cold as it was. Neither would Corey be playing handball on the patch of concrete against the back wall of the Yard that he and a couple of other prisoners painstakingly chipped clear of ice the day before. And Seth. Well, the young prisoner did not have a Yard routine yet. He walked around, that was about it. But Jonny was sure he would find something soon.

The light on the ceiling of their cell flickered on, and a blast of static came over the loudspeakers.

"Paddleboard Count! Report to the front of your cells and have your IDs ready!"

The announcement confirmed it. They were on lockdown. At that moment, every prisoner inside the Walls was locked in a cell. Except, perhaps, the dead one.

"FUCK YOU, PIGS!"

"WE WANT CHOW!"

"THIS IS BULLSHIT!"

Some prisoners shouted from their cells, and Jonny could hear more subdued grumbles of dissent from others around the block. Little Matt handed him their ID cards, and he set them in the bars.

Jonny had the car magazine open when the guards came by to count. There were three of them, followed by a sergeant dressed in tactical gear who Jonny had never seen before. One of the guards plucked their IDs off the bars and compared the pictures with the faces in the cell. The sergeant also looked in, hard-eyeing them. Jonny felt a surge of resentment well up inside him. What had they done to deserve the way this guy was looking at them? Were they supposed to be intimidated? Jonny wanted to say something, but he knew it would only get them sent to the Hole, so he held his tongue.

"Shooting that guy was bullshit," Jonny said, after the guards moved on.

"They didn't even fire a warning shot," Matt pointed out. "They've always fired one before."

"They fired one," Corey contradicted.

Jonny and Matt looked at their oversized cellie. "It was the second shot."

Corey erupted into laughter that lasted several seconds, until he broke it off when he realized that no one else was laughing.

"You guys are nigger lovers," he grumbled. "It was

his own fucking fault. He could have handled business in the cell and the Man never would have known. Instead, he took it out to the courtyard, right in front of the gun tower. How smart was that?"

Corey had a point. But Jonny had been around long enough to have a good sense of why the young prisoner had done what he had. He was scared. He did not want to fight the larger, more experienced prisoner in the cell they shared because there was no one there to step in if things went badly for him. In the courtyard, he figured that even if it went badly, guards would break it up before it got too ugly. The young prisoner had simply misjudged the kind of help the guards were there to give.

"I was in the *R Units* with him," Seth said.

"Who?" Jonny asked.

"The guy they shot. He came in on the same chain as me."

"What was he in for?" Matt asked.

"A dope beef. They gave him twenty-two months."

"Jesus Christ," Jonny swore. "Why'd they send him here?"

Seth shrugged. "It's where they classified him."

Jonny shook his head. "That's crazy. Putting a motherfucker behind the Walls with twenty-two months on a nonviolent drug charge—what the fuck is wrong with these people?"

"Look on the bright side." Corey suggested, drawing their attention back to him. "If he came in the same time you did," Corey pointed up at Seth, "that means he's got in what? Five or six months from the county, right?"

Seth nodded, unsure what Corey was getting at.

"Well," Corey continued, "he only did six months on twenty-two. That ain't bad." Corey laughed again, louder this time, although he cut it off again when he realized no one had joined him.

"You guys are nigger lovers."

"That isn't it," Jonny said. "It doesn't matter who it

was—the shit isn't right."

Jonny went to the wood shelf bolted to the end of his bunk and retrieved the empty peanut butter container he used for a drinking glass. Depressing a button on the steel sink at the back of the cell, he triggered a stream of water from its calcified tap. He pondered the pangs he felt in his stomach, wondering if they were really from hunger or if they had appeared because he could not keep from dwelling on the fact that they had not made it to chow. Either way, he thought drinking water would help. It was what he had done in IMU. In that place, there had been no question that the stabbing aches that pierced his shrunken belly were not imagined.

When the water had run for more than a minute, Jonny filled the jar. Holding it up to the light, he looked to be sure it was clear. At least as clear as it got in that place. When he was satisfied, he drank.

Jonny was struck by the roar of the rest of the cellblock coming in through the bars, in contrast to what was going on inside his cell. His cellies were quiet. Little Matt lay on his bunk writing in a notebook. And Corey had turned his attention back to the newspaper. On the bunk above him, Seth was reading too. Jonny noted with dismay that the younger prisoner had a bible.

Jonny believed that only ignorant prisoners put their faith in a bible. Or serial killers and rapos. He supposed that it was not the young prisoner's fault. Seth had just not been around long enough to see the same things Jonny had. The Hillside Strangler and The South Hill Rapist both petitioned for release from prison on the grounds they had turned their lives over to God and were changed. "Reborn," they called it. Presumably as a non-psychopathic killer and a non-rapist. Jonny thought that if that did not turn a person's stomach on God, nothing would. Seth would learn soon enough, he thought. And seeing the black kid shot in front of him was not a bad way for him to start. Jonny settled on a course of action—he would steal the bible in the morning and get rid of it on his way to work.

It was not that Jonny did not believe in God. He was not sure if there was one or not. But there was one thing he was sure of. If a god did exist, the extent of his realm did not reach inside those walls.

Jonny returned to his footlocker and sat down. “How was work?”

Little Matt’s pen halted its passage across the paper and he looked at Jonny. “Same as always.”

Jonny nodded. He had never worked in the license plate factory, but he knew it was a drudgery. Standing at a workstation repeating the same job day after day. No opportunity for advancement. Until the day when you don’t watch what you are doing carefully enough and your fingers or hand are crushed under a press or severed by a shear. Then they fire you.

“I go to classification review next month,” Matt said. “I’m going to ask for a transfer to the other side of the mountains.”

No surprise in that, Jonny thought. Any prison would be better than where they were. He knew that nearly every prisoner that went to their yearly review asked for a transfer, but few got it. Prison officials had to maintain a count at the prison, and they did not give them up easily. Unless, of course, it was in a body bag.

“Why you want to bail on us?”

Matt frowned. “I don’t think you need to worry, they aren’t going to move me anywhere.”

“What’s up with your appeal?”

Matt shook his head, holding onto his frown. “They’re not going to do anything for me on that either. I think the only person who still can’t see that is my dad. He can’t accept it, and he’s letting it override his good sense. He’s paying a lawyer who has convinced him he can get me out, but the guy writes briefs he knows aren’t going to go anywhere. Believe me, I read the crap he submits. It’s garbage. The truth is, they aren’t ever going to take back what they did. Taking it back would be admitting they were wrong, and they just aren't going to do that."

Jonny thought about what Matt said. He knew what he was seeing in his friend. He had seen it too many times in that place not to recognize it. Hope abandoned people in prison, although not always all at once. Most often, it departed piecemeal, disintegrating an increment at a time, worn away by attrition and disillusionment. Jonny knew this was the case with Matt. After ten years, he had progressed to the stage in which it had become real to him—he accepted that he would never get out. The only hope he could dredge up was the hope that perhaps someday he might be transferred to a better prison. Maybe one where it was not as likely that someone would be shot dead in front of him.

"I'm going to ask for Twin Rivers," Matt said. "It's close enough to my folks that I could get regular visits. I even heard that the cells there have windows in them that look out onto the Yard. Can you imagine?"

Someone began to rattle a cell door not far from them. "Y-A-A-A-R-R-R-D! WE WANT Y-A-A-A-R-R-R-D!"

The clanking of steel and shouting resounded throughout the cellblock, tapping into the mood of festering discontent. Others began to join in.

"Y-A-A-A--R--R--R-D!"

"GIVE US OUR FUCKIN' YARD, COPPERS!"

When one prisoner rattled his cell door, it was loud. When more than a dozen did it, the sound was like a freight train passing through the center of the cellhouse. Even the guards shut away in their office outside the block could not ignore it. Especially as more prisoners joined in. Jonny heard the loudspeakers click on as he went to the cell door and looked out.

"Knock it off!"

The announcement was hardly audible over the clamor. And it only caused the door rattling and yelling to grow immediately louder.

Jonny wanted to laugh. Knock it off? Is that all they had to say? They would have to do better than that, he thought.

A minute later, the cacophony subsided as quickly as it had begun.

"One time on A Tier," Jonny announced to his cellies, as he looked down on the guards who had come onto the bottom tier.

"Why yell for Yard?" Corey asked. "We should be yelling for dinner. When they give us that, then we can make them give us Yard."

"They aren't going to give us anything," Jonny said. "It don't matter how much we yell." The door rattling started again.

"Y-A-A-A-R-R-R-D!"

"Y-A-A-A-R-R-R-D!"

The noise lasted for several minutes before falling to a few sporadic fits of door clanging, then dying altogether. Jonny could no longer see guards on the bottom tier. Retrieving the mirror fragment, he held it outside the bars and looked down his own tier.

"They're handing out the mail," Jonny said. He saw a guard at the end of the tier setting letters in the bars of cellfronts as he passed.

Jonny's cellies remained quiet. All of them hoped to get something, he knew. No matter how unlikely the prospect.

As the guard drew closer to their cell, Jonny noted how much mail was in his hand. He wondered how unreasonable it would be to think there was a possibility that he would get a letter.

When the guard was four cells away, he spotted a blue envelope among the letters. It caught his attention because his mom sent letters in envelopes that color. He wondered what the chances were that someone else would get mail in that same kind of envelope.

When the guard arrived at the front of their cell, Jonny stepped back. His eyes remained on the blue envelope.

"James." The guard set a letter on the bars. "Morgan." He set another beside it.

After a brief shuffle through the remaining letters, the guard moved away. Jonny had to restrain himself to keep from saying anything. He wanted to call the guard back and ask him to check the name on the blue envelope. But he knew that he would only make himself feel like a fool if he did. No mail had come for him. He needed to face up to it. Handing Matt and Seth their letters, he concentrated on not letting it bother him.

Kicking off his boots, Jonny used the end of his footlocker as a step and leapt up onto his bunk. Laying down, he stared at the crack in the concrete ceiling directly above his face. It struck him that the guards had played them: no one was yelling or rattling their cell doors anymore. And Jonny knew why. Those who had gotten mail were busy reading it. Focused on words from home or elsewhere, their minds were for the moment not in that place. And those who had not gotten anything felt the same as Jonny did. Either way, no one felt like making noise anymore. Jonny realized the guards had control of them down to a science. He hated them for that.

"Hey."

Jonny turned away from the crack and looked at Corey.

"You're not trippin' because you didn't get mail, are you?"

"No."

Jonny's denial was too quick to be credible.

"You feel like getting beat up at some cards?"

Jonny shook his head. "I'm conserving energy so I don't starve to death."

"Laying there thinking about it only makes it worse."

Jonny knew Corey well enough to know that he would not leave him alone until he acquiesced, so he sat up.

"I'm not gambling. I don't have anything I can afford to lose."

Corey chuckled and rose from his bunk. He went to the back of the cell and began to dig around on his shelf.

Jonny did not forget that Corey was the one who had taught him years earlier that gambling was not his strong suit. And Jonny had taken the lesson to heart. At least when it came to gambling with Corey.

"Grab the cards out of my footlocker," Corey told him, as he shuffled through papers on the back table.

Jonny jumped down from his bunk and slipped into his shower shoes. Grasping the handle on the end of Corey's footlocker, he slid it out from beneath the bunk. When he lifted the lid, he froze.

Corey laughed.

"Where'd you get this stuff?"

Jonny stared down at a half-dozen packages of ramen, cheese, corn chips, a sausage, and a jar of jalapenos.

"You didn't think I spent all day working on those two kitchen workers for free, did you?"

Corey held up his hefty hand and Jonny slapped five with him. Collecting the food items out of the footlocker, they packed them to the back of the cell. As Jonny unloaded what he carried onto the table, he saw that Seth had lost interest in his letter and was watching them.

"You going to make the *donut*?" Corey asked.

Jonny nodded. He set to work unwinding the toilet paper, while Corey retrieved an empty two liter bottle with its top cut off and filled it with water. Setting the bottle on the narrow edge of the small sink, Corey lowered a *stinger* into it. It was a precarious setup, but the only place from which the stinger's short cord was able to reach the outlet.

Seth came down off his bunk, and Corey put him to work cutting up peppers with a razor blade. Matt joined them, busying himself gathering all their available plastic containers and washing them out.

Making the final twist of the donut, Jonny tucked the remaining toilet paper into the hole in its center, then paused to inspect his work. He knew he was better at this than anyone else in the cell, especially Corey, whose attempts were smoldering disasters that more than once had nearly got them sent to the Hole. When Jonny concluded it was as close to perfect as he could get it, he set the donut on the back of the steel toilet.

To anyone who did not live in that place, the back of a toilet would no doubt at first not appear to be the best place to cook. But the prisoners who lived there knew better. If a guard came onto the tier, this was where you wanted the donut—the flaming knot could be knocked quickly into the bowl and whisked away with a flush before the Man was any wiser. There was even a vent in the wall beside it that pulled the smoke out of the cell and into the plumbing chase between cellblocks. It was the best place for a fire.

Jonny watched as Corey removed the wire from one of Matt's spiral notebooks and straightened it. His cellie threaded it into the sausage, skewering the meat through from one end to the other. Beside him, Little Matt began to crush the packages of noodles and empty them into containers.

"I'll stand point," Jonny said, deciding the others could manage without him.

They were crowded into the back of the cell and there was no room to move. Jonny made his way around his cellies and went to the bars at the front of the cell. He knew it was not likely that any guards would be wandering the tiers after they handed out the mail, but they could not take that for granted. Not being careful was how prisoners landed in the Hole, pacing a tiny, airless cell wearing only undershorts. Two-and-a-half steps in one direction, and two and a half in the other.

Jonny looked down the tier through the mirror

fragment. No guards. Over the noise of the cellblock, he could hear a match being struck in back of the cell and knew it was being touched to the donut, where it would ignite a slender, long-burning flame. He studied the sausage packaging in his hand. The expiration date stamped on it had passed more than two years earlier, but that did not concern him. They had gotten other sausages like this out of the kitchen and had eaten them with no ill effect. He had to get rid of the packaging though. If guards found it in the cell, they would all catch write-ups for theft. Pushing it out through the bars, he tossed it over the side of the tier. Laying on the garbage-strewn tier three floors below, no guard would be able to pin it on them.

Jonny began to hear the pop and sizzle of the sausage roasting over the open flame. The aroma came to him strongly, sharpening the pangs in his stomach. He thought that they should have set up Matt's fan. Then he remembered that it no longer worked. Guards had broken it in a cell search a week earlier.

A curt whistle pierced the din of the cellblock, and Jonny returned his attention to the mirror fragment in his hand. A whistle like the one that had sounded meant that guards had entered the cellblock. Less than a minute later, he saw them at the end of the tier. He could not tell how many there were, but he saw enough to know it was not a routine tier walk. They were coming for someone.

"Cops." Jonny inflected urgency through his voice.

Corey kicked the flaming donut into the toilet and flushed. Jonny saw it relinquish a final puff of smoke before being sucked down. His cellies scrambled around in the back of the cell trying to get things out of sight.

Jonny took a last look through the mirror. The guards were halfway down the tier and still coming. Pulling his hand into the cell, he returned the mirror to the stash spot and picked up a section of newspaper from Corey's bunk. Taking a seat on the end of his footlocker, he pretended to read.

Corey hurriedly swiped a blanket through the air several times in an attempt to disperse the smoke. He sat down at the table just as the guards appeared in front of the cell.

Over the top of the newspaper that he held in front of him, Jonny counted five.

"What are you burning?"

It was the guard standing in front of the cell door who spoke. He was leading the squad and, to Jonny's chagrin, was the one who had conducted the strip search on him.

"Ain't nothing burning in here," Corey responded in his standard irreverent tone. The guard glared at him.

"Which one of you is Anderson?" Jonny lowered the paper.

"You?"

Jonny nodded.

"Turn around and cuff up."

The command did not surprise Jonny. He knew the only reason guards would come to the cell like this for him while they were on lockdown would be to take him to the Hole. He wondered if it was because of what he had said during the strip search. Considering everything else that had happened, it was hard to believe they would haul him away for that. But he could not think of anything else it could be. As he stood up, he saw Corey eyeing him questioningly.

"It's all right, bro," Jonny assured his cellie, letting him know that he would go with the guards

Whatever they were locking him up for, Jonny did not think it was serious. He would probably be out again in thirty days. At the same time, it felt good knowing that Corey would ride with him if he decided to make a stand. He had no doubt that if he believed the guards were there to jump him and he refused to cuff up, Corey would get down with him. So would Little Matt. And, he was certain, Seth had the heart for it too. Even though the outcome of resisting was inevitable—they would be gassed, shocked, beaten, and thrown in IMU for a long time. Jonny felt that being willing to stand with him and go to IMU for as long as they would be kept there was no different than being willing to die with him. Cellies just did not get any more solid than the ones he had.

Jonny took his coat off the bunk post and put it on, expecting to hear the guards order him not to. Everyone knew the rule. When they take you to the Hole, you go exactly as you are. But, for some reason, the guards did not say anything to him. Pushing his sleeves up, Jonny turned his back to the bars and held his arms out behind him. He would not ask what they were taking him to the Hole for. He knew the guards would not tell him anyway. Why give them the pleasure of denying the information?

A guard clapped cuffs on Jonny and cinched them tight, the steel as cold on Jonny's wrists as it was outside.

"The rest of you have to cuff up too."

Jonny moved aside so his cellies could be handcuffed as well. That was another rule. When the joint was on lockdown, everyone in a cell had to be cuffed before the door was opened. Each of his cellies took their turn at the bars and were placed in handcuffs.

"You three go to the back of the cell and face the wall while we take him out."

"Scared..." Corey grumbled loud enough for the guards to hear as he followed Matt and Seth to the back of the cell.

Jonny again turned his back to the bars, and one of the guards waved at the control booth. When the cell door began to open, hands grabbed him, taking control of his arms and the link between his cuffed wrists. They pulled him backwards out of the cell and held him on the tier while the door closed again and one of the guards uncuffed his cellies.

"Don't forget where you live, Jonny," Corey called

out as Jonny was prodded forward and began to move down the tier.

Jonny was careful to stay in step with the guards. He did not want them to wrench on the handcuffs, which is what they do to prisoners whose movement is not exactly what they want it to be. It never failed to evoke an instant flash of anger and resentment in him. No different than yanking the chain around a dog's neck in order to bully him into going where you want him to go. Anyone who resisted being jerked around in this manner was hauled away with cuffed wrists pulled high behind their back. Or they were thrown to the ground and beaten. Wanting to avoid that, Jonny concentrated on keeping the right pace. He was conscious that there were many ways in which he had been trained like a dog since coming to prison. This was one of them.

As they left the tier, Jonny again scoured his memory for why they might be taking him to the Hole. He did not believe it was for what he had said during the search. If they were going to do that, he was certain Lt. Todd would have ordered them to do it at the time. Not later. That was just the way he was.

At the top of the stairs, Jonny spotted Anton below on the ground floor, near the metal detector. He was in cuffs and faced away from them, a guard at each shoulder. Jonny thought that they must have found something in their shop. Why else would they lock them both up?

When Jonny reached the ground floor, a guard assigned to the cell-house called from the doorway of the duty office.

"Should I take them off the count?"

"They'll be back," one of the guards holding onto Jonny said. "They're going out for a cleanup at the Shift Office."

It was now clear to Jonny. They were going to work. Not to the Hole. The cuffs had thrown him off. But they were only in them because of the lockdown.

Anton was taken out the front door of the cell-house first. Jonny a dozen yards behind him. As he stepped out into the cold, Jonny wished that he had put his cap on before leaving the cell. It was in his pocket, but, with a guard holding onto each of his arms and handcuffs on, there was no way for him to don it at this point. He was also conscious of the pain in his stomach, which had become sharper than it was in the cell, as if his stomach were retaliating for having been tormented with the promise of food. He wondered how long they would be at the Shift Office. If he got back quickly enough, he might still be able to get a share of the food.

Near the Chowhall, Jonny again saw the dark patch on the ice. It looked black, but that was only because the yellow light that suffused the courtyard leached everything of its color. His eyes remained on the spot until they passed it.

They moved through the security gate and into Movement Control, the same building in which they had been searched on the way to work that morning. The distance between Jonny and Anton had closed and the guards holding onto Jonny's arms pulled him to a stop directly behind him. A door to their right clacked loudly as its locking mechanism was disengaged. It opened outward, and a disheveled old guard with a face like a bulldog's stepped out. He held the door as Jonny and Anton were ushered through and into the Shift Office, where they found the rat-face sergeant seated behind a desk.

Rat-Face looked up at them and smiled. It was an attempt at affability, Jonny supposed. Although he may as well have spit on them—the effect was the same.

"Go ahead and uncuff'em," the sergeant told the guards behind them.

When the handcuffs were removed, the guards filed out of the office, leaving Jonny and Anton alone with the sergeant and his pug-faced doorman. Jonny massaged his wrists where the steel had bitten into them and stole a glance at Anton, who did not return his look. Rat-Face addressed them.

"I've got a mess in the holding cell."

The sergeant paused as though anticipating a response. When none came, he continued. "You guys do a good job, and I'll have one of my officers pick you up a sack lunch from the Kitchen before we return you to your cells."

The sergeant was uncharacteristically cheerful and Jonny wondered why. Rat-Face knew as well as they did that he did not have to negotiate. If he ordered them to clean something up, they had to do it. Either that, or they would spend an interminable period without a job. Possibly years.

The sergeant nodded to his doorman. "Show 'em."

Jonny and Anton followed the guard into a corridor outside the office. The light-colored tiles in the hallway had been tracked with what Jonny immediately recognized was blood. He estimated that it had taken more than a dozen pairs of boots to make as many tracks as he saw. He wondered if the guards had brought the body through here. But that did not make sense. The infirmary was in a different section of the prison. He considered asking pug-face where the blood had come from but thought better of it.

The guard unlocked the hall's mop closet. "Knock when you're done."

These were the first words that Jonny and Anton had heard the guard speak, and he grumbled them as if he were angry. After he returned to the office and locked the door, Jonny and Anton looked at each other.

"What do you suppose is his problem?" Jonny asked.

Anton shrugged. "Hates prisoners, I suspect."

Unable to contain it, Jonny laughed. He was not sure why he thought Anton's response was funny. Because it was obvious perhaps. What else would the guard's problem be?

"Grab a mop and I'll go see what else we're going to need," Anton told him, bringing Jonny's attention back to what they were there for.

In the mop closet, Jonny set a bucket beneath the faucet and twisted open the basin's valve. As water began to thump against the bottom of the bucket, he thought he heard his crew leader call his name. Shutting off the water, he leaned out of the closet and looked down the corridor. Anton stood at the far end, in front of what Jonny knew was a holding cell, and waved for Jonny to come.

When Jonny reached the holding cell and looked in, he froze. "Jesus Christ."

Jonny was not conscious of the words he murmured. His attention was drawn fully to what he saw in front of him. Blood covered the floor of the bare six-by-fifteen-foot cell and was spattered and handprinted across the white-washed walls. He realized he was holding his breath, and he forced it to again move in and out. It disturbed him that he did not feel a sense of outrage. He had been around long enough to know what had taken place. His crew cleaned this cell once a week and he could not remember a time when they had not found some amount of blood or other remnant of violence there. But he was too tired to stir up a strong feeling. Not physically tired, but emotionally. His fatigue born from the knowledge that no matter what he managed to bring himself to feel—no matter what emotion he generated or how strong it was—it would not change anything. What he saw on the floor and walls in the cell was just the reality of life in that place. What he had always known it to be. Anyone who expected anything different was simply not in touch with the way things were there, how the prison was run.

"Who do you think it was?" Jonny asked.

"The Mexican. The one they hauled out of the courtyard after the shooting," Anton said, pointing to something on the floor of the cell.

Jonny followed the line of his finger and saw a thick clump of dark hair. There were several in the cell. Another reason to keep his head shaved, Jonny thought.

Jonny noted that much of the blood had dried, with the exception of the larger pools. Although even they had thickened. He knew blood was hardest to get up at this stage.

"We won't get out of here unless we get started," Anton said.

He was right, Jonny thought. Staring at it was not going to get it cleaned up. Pulling his gaze away from the cell, Jonny followed his crew leader down the hall to the mop closet.

They divided their effort. Anton set to work on the walls of the cell, and Jonny the floor. Jonny swept the hair up first and found two teeth in the process. One was a molar, and he wondered how the guards had knocked it out. His first pass with the mop did not accomplish much. He laid water down after that and let it soak into the areas where the blood had set. His next pass got a better result. When he finished the floor in the cell, he mopped the tracks in the corridor. He was not conscious of time as he worked. His attention remained on the work itself—what they had to get done in order to get out of there.

Jonny and Anton cleaned up in the mop closet. After they washed their hands and dried them on rags, Anton turned to Jonny.

"You ready?"

Jonny nodded, feeling suddenly tired. This time physically. He looked forward to going back to his cell. He knocked on the door of the Shift Office while Anton closed up the mop closet. Pug-Face opened the door.

"We're done," Jonny told the guard, noting that he still looked like he hated prisoners.

"You two are going to have to wait in the holding cell until I get an officer over here to take you back to your cell-house," Pug-Face said as he stepped into the hall.

Jonny and Anton followed the guard down the hallway toward the holding cell. As they did so, Jonny reflected on the ridiculousness of guards referring to themselves and each other as "officers." Even, sometimes, "corrections officers." The words weighed against his experience of prison. He supposed it was the guards' way to feel better about themselves, their attempt to define themselves as something other than what they were. But, the way Jonny saw it, they were propagating a lie. Changing the name of something did not change what it was. Especially in relation to that place and the things he had seen guards do there.

When Jonny and Anton entered the cell, the guard slammed the door shut behind them. Jonny knew the lock on the barred door was heavy, and the only way it could be closed was with force. But he still hated the sound. It felt as though it echoed inside him.

"How long will we have to stay in here?" Jonny asked, exerting himself to muster a civil tone.

Pug-Face did not answer. He pulled against the cell door in order to make sure it had locked.

Jonny knew that guards regarded questions like the one he had asked as absurd. When they locked a prisoner in a cell, he was going to be there as long as he was there. Simple as that.

When the guard left, Jonny shrugged. He knew better than to ask, and he was ashamed to have done it in front of his crew leader.

Anton felt the floor at the back of the cell with his hand in order to make sure it was dry. Satisfied that it was, he lowered himself onto it and laid down, clasping his hands behind his head and crossing his boots, soles faced in Jonny's direction.

"You might as well get comfortable."

Standing at the cell door, Jonny looked at his crew leader. "We probably won't be in here long."

"Didn't you see the clock when he came out of the

office?" Anton asked. "It's almost count-time. We're stuck in here until after shift-change."

Jonny pressed his back against the wall of the cell and let out a long, tired breath. He slid downward until he came to rest on the cold tile floor. Stretching his legs out in front of him, he leaned his head back until it, too, rested against the wall and he looked up. He saw a spattering of blood that Anton had missed above the door, but he did not say anything. What would be the point? He would try to remember it next time they called them out for a cleanup.

"Danny's coming back," Jonny said, allowing what was eating at him to spill out.

"The one that used to cell up with Claude and J.T.?"

"Yeah."

"Where'd you hear that?"

"It was in the paper."

Jonny took the stocking cap out of his coat pocket and put it on. He was not cold, but the hat made a good buffer between his head and the concrete wall.

"He'll probably get all day this time. They got him on some robberies."

"Good," Anton said, sounding as though he might be serious.

"That's not good. Why would you say that?"

"What?" Anton raised his head and looked at Jonny. "I liked Danny. He's a decent person. Why shouldn't I be glad he's coming back?"

They heard the door to the Shift Office open and voices approaching down the hall. Jonny caught sight of them just as he got his feet under him and was about to stand up. What he saw caused him to settle back onto the floor. Two guards with countboards stepped in front of the cell and looked in. Each marked their board, then moved off, disappearing as quickly as they appeared.

"Don't you think it would be better if he had stayed out?"

"Better for who?" Anton asked. "Not for me. I'm

glad for the company. The more the better. The way I see it, when they stuff enough of us in here and we all finally decide we're tired of it—that living in here like this is a whole lot worse than just plain dying—that's when we'll take this fucking place over and burn it down. That's the day I'm waiting for, Jonny—the day we stop this shit. The day we stop these motherfuckers from doing this to anyone else."

Anton was quiet a moment, then he continued.

"This place makes guys like Danny. They can't stay out."

Jonny felt a tendril of dread brush against his heart. "What do you mean?"

"I think they wreck us in here. Especially guys they send here when they are young, like Danny was, before they have any real experience living as an adult in the outside world. I came in as a teenager too—and I've never been out, so I can't speak on that. But I don't think the problem has anything to do with what's outside these walls—it's in here. Living like this fucks us up. So bad that it's hard for us to recognize it in ourselves.

Jonny wondered if he was fucked up. It had never before occurred to him that he might be. He felt normal.

"How does it fuck us up?"

"It's hard to pin down," Anton said. "It affects people in different ways. A person has to study himself carefully if he wants to figure out what it's done to him. There's one thing you can be sure of, it's done something. You have not been unaffected by it."

"What has it done to you?"

The words slipped out of Jonny of their own volition, he did not consciously form them. Nor would he, if he had thought about it. He respected Anton, nearly to a point of reverence. Who was he to ask him that? He wished he could take it back.

"I killed someone in a robbery, Jonny. That's what they sent me here for more than twenty years ago. The crazy thing about it was, I didn't mean to do it. I really didn't. It isn't something you can explain to anyone, they would have had to have been there to understand—how something like that can get away from you. I was an ignorant, young person who thought I was going to make my way in the world through crime. Because, up to that point in my life, that's the way I had always done it. I didn't know any other way. And I thought I was in control. But the truth is, you're never in control of a situation like the one it finally comes down to. Of course, by the time you recognize the consequence of it, it's too late. I'm not talking about the consequence of prison either. That's afterward. I'm talking about the moment it happens, the realization that with a single stab I took —no, stole—something from someone I could not give back. No matter how much I regretted it, Jonny. No matter how wrong I knew I was. They don't get it back.

"When they sent me here, I felt like I deserved it. I wanted to be punished. But I also wanted to live a different way. I wanted to try and reform myself into a different person—maybe a better person. In the state boys' homes and juvenile lockups I grew up in, I was surrounded by violence. And it wasn't different from me. I was a part of it. In those places, you don't have anything. You learn that the only way to get something, or hold onto whatever small thing you are able to acquire, is through violence. It didn't seem like a big deal, it was just the way things were. The problem was that it became my reaction to the world—to everything.

"But this place isn't any different, Jonny. It's always reminded me of a giant boys' home. A lie. What the state tells people outside these walls that prison is for, isn't what happens here. Living in here like this doesn't help us in any way make up for what we did. It doesn't help us change for the better. And the irony of it makes me sick. They sent me here for killing someone that I honestly didn't mean to. But, after living so long here, the truth now is that sometimes killing is all I think about. Like when I think of the guard who shot the kid in the courtyard tonight for no good goddamn reason. Or the pigs who run IMU. Or the ones who knocked out the teeth you found. It's when I think about these things that I realize how fucked up I am. A million times worse than before I came in."

Anton gazed up at the ceiling. Jonny noted the wrinkles at the corners of his eyes and thought it was strange that he had never noticed them before.

"I'm not coming back."

"I hope you do make it, Jonny." Anton's eyes remained fixed on the ceiling. "I hope you're the one. But if you aren't, I won't be disappointed."

A quiet fell over the holding cell. Neither Jonny or Anton said anything more, each retreating instead into his own thoughts. Sometime later they heard the Shift Office door open. Neither of them moved to get up.

"Sanchez, what's up?" Jonny asked the guard who appeared in front of the cell. The guard seemed surprised to see them.

"How long you guys been in here?"

Anton sat up and shrugged. "Could have been a couple days for all we know. They brought us over for a cleanup, then locked us in."

The guard shook his head. "They didn't say anything. I'm glad I came back to check."

Jonny and Anton got to their feet as the guard unclipped a key ring from his belt and began to flip through keys. Settling on one, he inserted it in the door's lock.

"What about cuffs?" Anton asked.

"We're off lockdown," the guard told them as he turned the oversized key in the lock and swung the barred door open.

Outside the cell Jonny and Anton turned toward the Shift Office.

"Let's go out this way," the guard told them, nodding toward a door at the opposite end of the hall. "Every asshole on night shift is in that office right now."

The guard's words reminded Jonny of why it was

that he had liked Sanchez ever since the first time he met him. He did not act like a guard.

The door the guard let them through opened onto the courtyard and, as they stepped out, Jonny felt the cold bite immediately into his face. The pain in his stomach was sharper. Sitting on the floor of the holding cell, he had made peace with it. But walking around, it was harder to ignore.

"You guys want to stop by the Kitchen and see what we can dig up?" The guard asked, seeming to read Jonny's mind.

The Kitchen was deserted. Entering through a side door, it struck Jonny that he had never seen it like this before. Whenever they went there for a cleanup, it was chaos, bustling with prisoners moving everywhere and the hiss of open steam valves overriding the banging of pans and shouted orders. It seemed strange like this.

"You guys know where they keep the lunches?" The guard asked.

"In back," Anton said, setting off across the Kitchen.

Jonny and the guard followed, moving past rows of steel counters and a line of giant steam kettles. At the back of the Kitchen they found a table with a dozen sack lunches on it. Jonny knew each contained the standard prison fare: a bologna sandwich and a green orange. Enough to keep a prisoner from starving.

Instead of taking a sack from the table, Anton went to a wall of nearby shelves and began to search through boxes. Settling on one, he tilted it toward Jonny and the guard so they could see what was inside.

"Chocolate chip," Anton said.

Jonny and Anton each emptied a sack of its contents and began to fill it with cookies. Jonny could tell they were made earlier that day. They had not yet hardened completely.

The guard laughed as Jonny unloaded a handful from the box. "I bet they'll hide them better next time," he said.

"You want a bag?" Anton asked, turning to the guard.

"That would probably be better than if I filled my pockets."

It was Anton's turn to laugh. "You sure you're a guard, Sanchez? Sometimes I think you're one of us in a stolen uniform."

"If the guys back in the neighborhood I grew up in knew I was a guard, they'd beat my ass. I could have as easily ended up in here, same as you guys. I try not to forget that."

It did not get past Jonny that Sanchez did not refer to himself as an officer. In fact, he had never heard him do it.

"I would work somewhere else if I could," the guard continued. "As soon as my kids—"

"You don't have to explain," Anton told him.

The guard shook his head. "I shouldn't be doing this. My uncle pulled a bit in California." Jonny and Anton looked at each other.

"How long?" Anton asked.

"Fifteen."

The number hung heavy between them for a moment.

"I can't help but wonder if this is what it was like for him. This place does something to people. You can feel it. And not just to you guys. It does something to the people who work here too."

The guard shook his head.

"It's not good. This isn't good for anybody."

"Where's your uncle now?" Anton asked.

The guard's face lit with a half-smile. "Idaho. He's married and doing pretty good. I take the kids up a lot of weekends and we fish together."

A silence fell between them that made Jonny uncomfortable in a way he could not put his finger on. He considered saying something, but did not. What could he say?

Anton pushed the box of cookies away and folded the top of one of the bags he had filled. A thought came to Jonny as he watched his crew leader hand the bag to the guard. When the day came that Anton told him about in the holding cell, he knew Sanchez was one guard who was going to be all right. Anton would make certain of it.

As they left the Kitchen, Jonny slipped the bag of cookies he had filled for himself inside his coat. He was comforted by the weight of it. He and Anton parted company with Sanchez outside the front of the cell-house.

Jonny was grateful they did not see any guards as they entered the building. Following Anton, he bypassed the metal detector and headed directly for the stairs. On the second landing, his crew leader stopped and turned to him.

"See you tomorrow, little brother." They clasped hands.

"See you tomorrow."

Jonny took the remaining stairs three at a time. The cellblock was quiet when he entered, and he wondered how long he had been gone. He sensed that it was late. The door of his cell opened before he reached it.

Matt and Seth were asleep, but Jonny found Corey still awake. His cellie was sitting up in his bunk with the light from a small reading lamp shining down on him. He was reading the newspaper. Jonny saw that he had made it to the classifieds.

"It was a cleanup," Jonny said, speaking quietly in order not to disturb his two sleeping cellies. He set the bag of cookies on the table at the back of the cell.

"I wasn't trippin'," Corey told him. "I knew you wasn't going to the Hole."

Jonny smiled, remembering the look on Corey's face when the guards had shown up and ordered him to cuff up. Taking his stocking cap off, he slipped it into the pocket of his coat and hung the coat on the post at the end of his bunk. He noticed both laundry buckets had dirty clothes in them.

"Where's the mouse?"

"I let him go."

"I thought you two hit it off. What happened?"

Corey lowered the paper. "Keeping him in that bucket felt too much like what they do to us. I couldn't do it."

Jonny sat down on the end of his footlocker. "Was his fur still sticking straight out when he left?"

Corey nodded, smiling at the thought.

"You did him wrong," Jonny said. "The other mice are going to laugh their asses off when they see him."

Corey's expression turned serious. "I was thinking about what you asked earlier."

Jonny looked at his cellie, not sure what he was referring to.

"I'll teach you how to cook if you still want me to."

Jonny's spirit buoyed immediately. The stress that had plagued him for most of the day lifted as he listened to his cellie.

"I'll teach you where to get the chemicals you'll need and how to set up a lab. By the time you get out, you'll be ready to roll."

Jonny's tired body felt charged. "Thanks."

Corey dropped the newspaper onto the floor next to his bunk and reached behind him to switch off the lamp.

"See you in the morning."

Pulling the prison-issue blanket over as much of himself as it would cover, Jonny's oversized cellie turned and faced the wall.

"Yeah, see you in the morning," Jonny whispered as he pulled loose the laces of his boots.

Jonny could smell the heavy dank funk of his socks as soon as the boots were off, and he regretted that he could not wash them. But he was not the kind of guy to splash water around in the sink in the middle of the night and wake up his cellies. He hung the socks, which had been his last clean pair when he put them on that morning, off the end of his bunk. He would wear them again the next day.

Climbing up onto his bunk, Jonny was careful not to disturb Matt. He found a plastic container of food awaiting him, and he smiled to himself. His cellies had saved him a share after all. Sitting cross-legged, he leaned back against the wall and picked up the make-shift bowl. He thought of others he had celled with over the years, an endless stream of faces, and he realized that he would not trade any of them for Corey, Matt, or Seth. Removing the lid from the container, he dug into the cold hash of ingredients and began to eat.

When Jonny finished, the comforting weight of the food filled his belly and he felt a sudden tiredness descend upon him. He slipped out of his clothes without getting off the bunk. Pulling his blanket over him, he looked up at the crack in the ceiling. He remembered a countless number of other nights he had stared at this same jagged seam of concrete, each night hoping the following day might in some way be better than the one that preceded it. It was that hope that had gotten him this far through his stretch—what gave him the strength to continue on even at the worst of times in that place. He was conscious that this night was different, though, as he reflected back on the day.

When he awoke that morning, he had thought he might be sick. But he no longer believed that.

He saved a mouse.

He made it past the guard at the front of the cell-house with the Mexican's shank.

He earned four packs of tobacco.

He ate, even though they had not made it into the Chowhall. And he scored a bag of cookies.

But most importantly, he talked Corey into teaching him how to cook dope. It was this last achievement that filled him with the greatest sense of wellbeing, an assuredness that everything would be all right after all.

Jonny fell asleep fully content that night, without the delusion that the next day might in some way be better. No matter what happened the next day, or any day after, he knew the memory of how good it had been this day would see him through.

Epilogue

Jonny set the pen down. His hand ached, but he felt good. This was it. The day he remembered most from his last stretch in prison. He had not made it outside those walls long before they sent him back broken off, although a number of things had happened while he was gone.

Seth was dead. The youngster had opted to cheat the state out of its time by hanging himself with a filthy prison sheet on the same tier in the Hole that Jonny was on now.

Corey was in IMU after being ratted out for one of his hustles. So far he had lost more than a 100 pounds.

Little Matt moved to another cell but was still in Eight Wing. Still stamping out license plates for the state.

And Anton's girl finally tired of waiting for the miracle that would get her man out and allow him to come home to her. Settling for someone easier to come by, she had stopped coming to see him.

Anton, on the other hand, was still waiting for his day. Not a day when he imagined he would somehow be able to get out of prison. His heart had long since given up such a ridiculous notion. The day he waited for was the one in which they would rise up, take this godforsaken place over, and burn it to the ground.

This is the day Jonny now waits for too.

Glossary

all day: A sentence that will take longer to complete than the prisoner who received it can possibly live.
Bay, the: A familiar appellation for Clallam Bay Corrections Center, one of Washington State's closed-custody prisons.
beef: The charge (or charges) a prisoner is convicted of.
broke off, broken off: (See "all day")
cellie: Someone you share a cell with.
chain bus, the: A fortified prison transfer bus.
DOC: Washington State Department of Corrections.
donut: Tightly bound ring of toilet paper that, when lit, is used to cook food or sterilize tattoo needles, etc.
duck: A newly arrived prisoner who is in prison for the first time.
5 - 0 (five - oh): Heads-up signal between prisoners that a guard is approaching.
freeworld: The world outside the prison walls. Prisoners conceptualize this in varying degrees of abstraction, in accordance with how long they have been in prison and how young they were when they were sent there.
good-time (good-time credit): Number of days a month a prisoner can earn for being free of disciplinary infractions.
holiday: A patch or area of floor unintentionally left uncoated with wax.
Hole, the: A segregated, high-security cellhouse in which prisoners are kept in solitary confinement.
house: A cell.
IMU (Intensive Management Unit): The highest security section of a prison, used to house prisoners on indefinite, long-term solitary confinement. More severe than the Hole.
ISO (Isolation Status): A designation assigned to a prisoner by a disciplinary hearings lieutenant in order to make the prisoner's time more difficult than it already is. Prisoners on ISO are not allowed to possess

anything to read. They are afforded only one privilege, a five-minute shower once every three days only after they first strip and kneel for the guards.
keep point: To watch for the guards.
kick in: A cell search conducted by a team of guards.
MRSA (Methicillin-resistant Staphylococcus aureus) infection caused by a type of staph bacteria resistant to many antibiotics. MRSA is more common in crowded living conditions.
mayate: Hispanic prisoners' appellation for black prisoners.
one time: (See "5-0")
PC (Protective Custody): A segregated cell-house inside the Walls used to house prisoners who cannot live in the prison's General Population.
pruno: Prison-made alcohol.
Rapo: A prisoner convicted of any type of sex offense.
R Units: Receiving and reception center. Centralized Washington State prison where prisoners are sent upon conviction in order to be classified and assigned to a prison.
snipe hunting: Picking up discarded cigarette butts to smoke later.
stinger: Small electric immersion heater sold on prison commissaries.
strip-cell: A cell that contains nothing (no mattress pad, sheets, blankets, running water) into which a prisoner is placed naked. If it is the prisoner's first offense, he will spend ten days there. If not, he will be there longer.
stuck: To be stabbed.
toad: White prisoners' appellation for a black prisoner.
Walls, the: A familiar appellation for the Washington State Penitentiary.

About the Author

Arthur Longworth was born in Tacoma, Washington, was state-raised, and entered prison at the age of 21 with a seventh-grade education. He has written for *The Marshall Project*, *Vice News*, and *Yes Magazine*, and is the recipient of three National PEN Awards. *Zek* is his first novel. For more, visit www.arthurlongworth.com.

CPSIA information can be obtained
at www.ICGtesting.com
Printed in the USA
LVHW050130270220
648278LV00007B/217